THE ROAD TO DEATH

"Map . . ." the man said, his voice growing faint. "Don't tell anyone . . . don't let anyone get it . . . yours now . . ."

"Hey, friend . . . hey!" Clint said, but it was too late. The man's eyes closed and Clint could *feel* the life run out of his body.

He was holding a dead man . . .

THE Gunsmith

138

DEADLY GOLD

J. R. ROBERTS

JOVE BOOKS, NEW YORK

DEADLY GOLD

A Jove Book / published by arrangement with
the author

PRINTING HISTORY
Jove edition / June 1993

ISBN: 0-515-11121-X

Jove Books are published by The Berkley Publishing Group,
200 Madison Avenue, New York, New York 10016.
The name "JOVE" and the "J" logo
are trademarks belonging to Jove Publications, Inc.

PRINTED IN THE UNITED STATES OF AMERICA

10 9 8 7 6 5 4 3 2 1

ONE

Sacramento, California, had become one of Clint Adams's favorite cities. The main reason was that it reminded him of San Francisco while not being nearly as crowded as that city.

He'd discovered in Sacramento that he was able to find all the same comforts—and vices—that he could find in San Francisco. One of those comforts was sleeping next to him right at that moment— or was Pat Kelly one of those *vices*? Were *women* vices or comforts? He couldn't be sure. Sometimes he was sure that they were vices, and other times they were definitely comforts. Whichever they were, however, when they looked like Patsy Kelly, and had as much energy and generosity as she did, they were wonderful creatures to be with.

So here he was in Sacramento with Patsy Kelly, and right at that moment life couldn't have gotten very much better.

It could only get worse.

To Mike Smith, Sacramento was a death sentence. *Staying* there meant death, but he might very well get killed trying to leave.

Smith stared out his window at the dark streets below. He was staying in a flea-bitten hotel close to the Sacramento docks because he dared not stay anywhere where the lights were too bright.

Smith was not a man who was easily noticed. At thirty-five, he was barely five feet four and weighed about one hundred and twenty pounds. He had grown up constantly fighting because of his height—or *lack* of it. All of his life had been spent trying to *act* taller, trying to find something that would *make* him taller. He'd thought he'd found it with this piece of paper, but now it wasn't turning out that way. Instead of making him taller, this piece of paper was going to end up making him dead.

He turned and walked to the rickety, flat-mattressed bed and sat down. From his pocket he took the folded-up piece of paper that was the source of all his problems. If he could, he would willingly give it up to save his life, but things had gone well beyond that. Whether he gave it to them willingly or not, the people who wanted it also wanted him dead, because he knew what was on that piece of paper.

He stared at it, and his hands began to shake uncontrollably. What would happen, he wondered, if he simply tore it to shreds, or *burned* it up? Would *that* make a difference to anyone?

Probably not.

It was probably true that no matter *what* he did, he was destined to be a dead man very, very soon.

Could things get any worse?

Clint turned the sheet down from Patsy as she lay peacefully on her back. Her breasts were like two hard, ripe peaches, and her flesh glowed the way only the young glowed. Patsy Kelly was probably twenty-two years old, give or take a year either way. Either way, she sure shouldn't be lying here with a broken-down old wreck like him—except when he was with Patsy he didn't feel like a broken-down old wreck. It was funny, but she made him feel young and alive again.

It was only lately that Clint Adams had started feeling his age. It happened once in a while, and it always corresponded with the beginning of spring. What was it about the early days of spring—the *young* days—that made him feel old? He tried to think back to the other times he'd felt like that. Had he sought out a young woman each time to help him combat the feeling? He couldn't remember. What was it they said, the memory was the first to go?

He stared at Patsy's breasts, and then reached out and touched one nipple with the tip of his forefinger. It felt hard and almost rubbery. He touched the other one, and it felt the same. He stroked one breast then, enjoying both the smooth *and* firm feel of the flesh.

Patsy stirred just a little as he stroked the other breast, and then she moaned when he pinched her left nipple between his thumb and forefinger. When he leaned over, took the nipple into his mouth, and sucked, she groaned and moved her legs. When he slid his hand down over her belly, through the forest of black pubic hair, and then deftly slipped one finger into her, she moaned and bit her bottom lip and spread her legs wide.

He inserted a second finger, then found her clitoris with his thumb and began to stimulate her that way.

"Oooh, God," she said, rubbing her firm butt

against the sheet, "am I awake or dreaming?"

Into her ear he said, "You're dreaming."

"Really?" she said, smiling with her eyes still closed. "If that's the case, don't *ever* let me wake up!"

TWO

Patsy Kelly was not a morning person. That was because Patsy was a waitress, and she usually worked late afternoon and evening shifts. The mornings, she said, were for sleeping. Lately the mornings—*and* the evenings—had been for making love with Clint Adams, but *after* the sex the mornings were still for sleeping.

That was why, at eight A.M., Clint Adams was walking the streets of Sacramento alone.

During an earlier trip to the city Clint had found himself a restaurant he really liked for breakfast. They served a lousy lunch and dinner, but when it came to greasy eggs and potatoes, bacon, and good, strong, black coffee, Cafe Adventure couldn't be beat.

Clint thought that they called it Cafe Adventure because it was an adventure to eat there.

The only drawback to the restaurant was its location. It was on a street very near to the docks, and so its clientele was mostly . . . questionable. In fact, Clint wouldn't have been surprised if it wasn't a prime location for some strong shanghai activity. He wasn't worried, though, because he was too damn *old* to work on a ship. And besides, the owner had come to know him and—

5

he thought—genuinely like him.

"Clint," Eddie Maple said as he entered, "back for breakfast again."

"What a surprise, right, Eddie?" Clint said, laughing. "Only the fourth time this week, right?"

"And it's only Friday," Maple said.

Maple was an ex-seaman who was now too old to work at sea. In his fifties, he had skin like rawhide from constant exposure to the elements. He had lines in his face that Clint was *sure* would hide a dime—and maybe even a quarter. His hands were gnarled and knotted from years of handling ropes and cargo. Eddie Maple owned the restaurant, but he was not the cook. His wife, Estelle, did the cooking. Estelle Maple was a surprise to anyone who met Eddie for the first time. They would never expect his wife to be a handsome woman in her late thirties who was *taller* than her husband's five-eight. Eddie and Estelle had been married for five years, however, ever since Eddie had given up the sea for the restaurant business, and they were very happy together. She had been his woman in port for over fifteen years, but had refused to marry him until he gave up the sea—or *it* gave *him* up.

"Same?" Eddie asked.

"Same," Clint said.

He sat down at his usual table. It was against a wall, but from it he could see out the window. He would have liked to sit by the window sometimes, but a man with his past could not afford such a luxury. Sitting by the window would be like painting a target on his forehead and saying, "Here it is, one free shot."

He was satisfied to have the wall at his back, and be able to see out the window from there.

He liked watching the people go by early in the morning. He often tried to guess where they might be going, and what they did for a living. He found it relaxing.

He had no way of knowing that on *this* morning, it would be anything *but* relaxing.

Mike Smith finally decided he couldn't stay cooped up in the hotel forever. He'd die of starvation if he tried to stay in his room. He decided to chance going down the street to the Cafe Adventure for breakfast. If he ran into the three men who were looking for him—*chasing* him, actually—he'd have to try to talk his way out of it. He'd give them the map, and try to convince them to let him live. He was *that* tired of running and hiding that he was willing to give it a try.

Eddie brought Clint's pot of coffee to the table, and over the first cup Clint watched the people going by outside, both on this side of the street and, if he craned his neck, across the street as well.

Over his second cup three men on this side of the street caught his eye. It wasn't that they looked out of place. They fit in well with this part of the city, all right, but there was something in their manner that made him watch them more intently. In fact, *they* seemed to be watching for someone—or *looking* for someone.

They stood just outside the restaurant, craning their necks and speaking to each other occasionally. It was possible that they were meeting someone they were going to have breakfast with, but they didn't look like the types to be meeting *anyone* for a leisurely breakfast.

Suddenly, the one in the middle nudged the other two and they all looked across the street. Hurriedly, they stepped down off the boardwalk and ran across the street. Clint had to stand up to see what happened next, but he was just curious enough to do it.

He saw a diminutive man across the street who tried to run when he saw the other three coming. He held his hands out to them, as if pleading, and then two of them grabbed him.

Clint moved away from the table and towards the window to get a better look.

The small man was talking very quickly, and his eyes were wide with fright. Clint could almost *smell* the fear in the air. The man was afraid for his life, but instead of running he was *talking*. Was he pleading for his life? Or were these friends of his who were simply playing a deadly game?

It wasn't until one of the other men took out a knife that Clint decided to intervene. He moved away from the window as the other two men tightened their hold on the small man, and the third man moved closer.

As Clint came out the door he saw the third man hitting the small, helpless man, and then he saw the knife flash in the early morning sunlight.

"Hey!" he shouted, but he was too late. All of his reactions this morning had been too late to do the small man any good. He'd been just a step too slow. Now he was stepping off the walk and running across the street.

The three men started to go through the small man's pockets, but as they saw Clint approaching—and as other people on the street started to notice what was happening—they released the man and ran.

The small man slumped to the ground, moaning and clutching at his belly. As Clint reached him he could see the ribbons of blood running through the man's fingers, and he knew the wound was bad.

"Damn it," Clint said, leaning over the man. "I'm sorry."

The apology was out of his mouth before he knew it, or could explain it. What did he have to be sorry about? How could he have known that the intention of the three men was to kill the smaller one?

"Help me . . ." the man said.

Clint grabbed him by the shoulders, and tried to support his head.

"Here . . ." the man said. He took one hand away from his belly wound to reach into his pocket. He came out with a piece of folded paper and pushed it into Clint's hand. "Here . . . take this . . . help me . . . don't let them get it . . ."

Instead of trying to cover the wound again with that hand, the man grabbed hold of Clint's arm and held it with surprising strength.

"What is it?" Clint asked, holding the paper but not looking at it. It was sticky with the man's blood.

"Map . . ." the man said, his voice growing faint. "Don't tell anyone . . . don't let anyone get it . . . yours now . . ."

"Hey, friend . . . hey!" Clint said, but it was too late. The man's eyes closed and Clint could *feel* the life run out of his body.

He was holding a dead man.

THREE

"I should have moved faster," Clint said, "done something sooner."

"Most people wouldn't have done anything, sir," the policeman said.

There were two of them, wearing uniforms. They would take down the information and make arrangements for the body to be removed. Someone else, they said, would be questioning him later. He gave them his name and the location of his hotel.

"If you're staying at that hotel," the other policeman, ten or twelve years older than the first, said, "what were you doing in this neighborhood?"

"I eat breakfast across the street," Clint said.

"Often?" the second policeman asked.

"Very often."

The first policeman closed his notebook and said, "Someone will be talking to you today, Mr. Adams."

"All right," Clint said.

"Thanks for your help."

"Yeah," Clint said glumly, "sure."

He took one last look at the dead little man, and then crossed back over to the restaurant.

The map, bloody and folded, was burning a hole in his pocket. He wasn't really sure why he hadn't given it to the police, or mentioned it, except that the little man had seemed desperate for him to take it.

When he reached the restaurant Eddie Maple was standing in the doorway.

"Still want your breakfast, Clint?" he asked.

"Nah, Eddie," Clint said, "I think I lost my appetite. Thanks."

"Hey," Eddie Maple said, "you did what you could. You can't blame yourself."

As Clint Adams walked away, a man joined the group of people who were trying to get a look at the body, and the blood. The man moved closer to one of the two policemen.

"Real helpful fellow," he said.

The younger of the two policemen turned and looked at the man.

"That he was," the policeman said.

"Not like others, huh?"

"Most people would have just watched, or walked away," the young policeman said. He waved an arm, encompassing all of the gawkers in the area, and added, "They don't come around until it's all over, and then they just want to stretch their necks and look. Most of them just want to see some blood."

"Guess that makes that fellow pretty special, huh?" the man asked.

"I'd say so," the policeman said. "At least he tried to do something to *keep* blood from being shed."

"You know, I think I know who he is," the man said. "His name's . . . um, what is it . . . Ben something, isn't it?"

"Ben?" the young policeman said, frowning. "No, that's not his name. His name is . . ." He consulted his notebook. "Adams, Clint Adams."

"I could swear his name was Ben. Oh, well, I must have been thinking about somebody else. I wonder what he was doin' down here."

"That's what my partner wanted to know," the policeman said. "Hell, he's staying at the White Palace Hotel. What was he doing coming down here to eat?"

"Probably slumming," the man said, and melted away into the crowd before the policeman knew it.

He'd gotten what he wanted.

FOUR

When Clint returned to the hotel Patsy was already gone. He assumed that she had gone back to her own bed for the rest of her sleep. She'd probably figured that when he returned she wouldn't be able to sleep anyway. As it turned out, that probably wasn't true. As much as Clint had lost his appetite for breakfast, he also had no appetite at that moment for sex.

He sat on his bed and took out the bloody piece of paper the man had given him.

Most of the blood was on the back, and while it had soaked through, it had not obliterated what was on the front. He spread it out and studied it. It appeared to be a map of the Shasta County region that was north of San Francisco. It took him only a few moments more to realize that it was apparently a treasure map—a map that led to a *gold* mine.

"Jesus!" he said angrily.

He flung the bloodied map to the floor. A man had lost his life for that? A phony map? What a waste!

He stared at the map for a few moments, then bent over and retrieved it. For want of something better to do with it, he refolded it and tucked it underneath the mattress. The little man had seemed so *desperate* for him to take it, not to let *them* get it. He assumed that the *them* referred to the men who had killed him.

He closed his eyes and tried to picture the three men as he had seen them through the window. Hell, if he had known they were going to commit *murder* he would have paid even more attention to them. The police were definitely going to ask him to describe them.

He could remember trail clothes, like they were cowhands in town after a drive, or just drifters. They had all worn guns, although none of them had ever made a move towards them. They had probably wanted to avoid attracting attention as long as possible. Damn, they would have gotten the map if Clint hadn't started running across the street shouting.

And they probably *still* wanted the map . . . but why? It *had* to be a phony map. There was no more gold in Shasta County. That region had played out long ago. The Chinese had gotten whatever little might have been left over. Why kill a man over it?

Clint decided that what he *did* need was a drink. Even though it was early, he thought he could go down to the dining room and convince somebody to get him a beer. He had made friends with most of the hotel personnel over the past week or so. Although the White Palace was considered a fine hotel, it was still small enough so that he knew most of the staff by now.

He left his room and went downstairs.

"His name's Clint Adams," Ken Hill said. "He's staying at the White Palace Hotel."

"Where did you get that information from?" Sam Dorn asked.

"From one of the policemen."

"He just *told* you who the guy was and where he was staying?" the third man, Carl Hamm, asked.

"That's right," Hill said. "Hey, you gotta know how to talk to people, to get them to talk to you."

"And you're such a goddamned expert on that, right?" Dorn asked.

"Sure, he is," Hamm said. "That's why he killed Smith before he could give us the map."

"Shit," Hill said, "that wasn't my fault. How was I supposed to know he'd be stupid enough to actually have it on him?"

"Well, he did," Dorn said. "We *saw* him give it to this fella Adams, before *you* made us run away."

"Hey," Hill argued, "the last thing we needed was a gunfight right in the middle of the street, in front of witnesses."

"So now there's only one witness we have to worry about," Hamm said. "This fella Adams. *He* can tell the police what we look like."

"And *he* most likely has our map," Dorn said.

"*Our* map?" Hill asked. "Come on, Dorn, it's not *our* map. It was Smith's map, and we was gonna take it away from him."

"So all we got to do is get it from Adams," Hamm said.

"And kill him," Dorn said.

"Right," Hill said, "that's all."

Except that Hamm and Dorn obviously didn't recognize Clint Adams's name the way Hill did. Hill *knew* they were going to have to go up against the Gunsmith to get that map, but he figured the reward would be worth the risk.

Besides, there were *three* of them and only one of him. He'd take those odds any day.

FIVE

Clint got Ted Grant to open the saloon for him. After all, it *was* only three hours early.

"Mr. Adams?"

Clint was standing at the bar with a beer. He turned and saw a man standing in the doorway that led from the dining room to the saloon. He was a tall, well-dressed man in his forties with gray-streaked black hair.

"Yes?"

The man walked in, looked around, and said, "It's a little early to open the saloon, isn't it?"

"The saloon's not really open," Clint said. "The manager's a friend of mine, so he let me in. I needed a beer."

"I see," the man said.

"Can I do something for you?" Clint asked.

"I hope so," the man said. "My name is Jack Gates—Lieutenant Jack Gates. I'm with the Sacramento Police Department."

"Oh . . . Lieutenant," Clint said. He wondered if Ted Grant was going to get in trouble for opening the saloon early.

"Well . . . since the saloon isn't really open," Gates said, "do you suppose I could have a beer as well?"

"Oh . . . well, sure," Clint said. "I'll get it for you."

He went around to the other side of the bar and drew the lieutenant a beer. He set it down on the bar, and then pulled his own beer over to him, remaining behind the bar.

"I suppose you want to talk to me about what happened this morning," he said.

"That's right," Gates said. "I read the report written by the men who were on the scene. Naturally, since I wasn't there I'll probably ask some questions you've already answered. I hope you don't mind."

"No, not at all," Clint said. "I'll do what I can to help."

"I understand that's what you were trying to do this morning," Gates said. "Why don't you tell me what happened from the beginning."

Clint explained how he had spotted the three men through the window of the restaurant, and then went on to outline the rest of the incident.

"And he died while you were holding him, eh?" Gates asked.

"That's right."

"Did he, uh, say anything to you before he died?" Gates asked.

"He . . . asked me to help him," Clint said, thinking about the bloody map in his pocket. Should he take it out and give it to the lieutenant?

"He didn't . . . give you anything, did he?" Gates asked.

"Give me anything?" Clint asked. "Like what?"

"Oh, I don't know," Gates said. "I just thought . . . you know, three men beating up one, and then killing him. Could it be they were after something?"

"I don't know," Clint said, studying the other man closely. There was something familiar about him.

Suddenly, the man threw the contents of his beer mug into Clint's face. Clint closed his eyes and raised his arm, but the damage was done. By the time he opened them the man was pointing a gun at him.

"I want that map," Gates—or rather, Sam Dorn—said.

Clint wiped his face on his sleeve and stared at the man.

"What map . . . Lieutenant?"

"Okay," Dorn said, "so I'm not a lieutenant. I'm not even a policeman."

"I guessed that by now," Clint said, cursing himself for being so stupid. It was much too soon for a police lieutenant to be looking for him. He doubted that the two policemen had even gotten back to the police station yet. He was so down on himself for letting the little man die that he was now in the position of letting *himself* be killed—and all over a stupid phony *map*. Why didn't he just give it to this man and be done with it?

"But I still want that map," Dorn said.

"Why?" Clint asked. "There's no gold left in Shasta County. Why the hell would you kill one man—or *two*—over a worthless map?"

"It's not worthless," Dorn said. "Now give it to me, or I'll kill you."

"If you pull that trigger in here," Clint asked, "how do you expect to get away?"

He saw the man's eyes shift as he realized what Clint was saying was true.

"You'll never get out of this hotel if you pull the trigger," Clint went on. "You might as well turn around and walk out now."

He saw the man consider the suggestion, and then shake his head.

"I can't," Dorn said. "Not without that map."

Clint shrugged and said, "Then pull the trigger."

He had one advantage over the man—well, two really. First, his gun was below the level of the bar, so that the other man couldn't see it. And two, *he* didn't care if the whole hotel heard a shot.

"Come on—" the man said, but it was too late for *him*. Clint drew his gun, and before the man knew what was happening he fired. The bullet struck Dorn in the center of the chest, and blood blossomed like a big red rose.

SIX

This time when the lieutenant from the Sacramento Police Department arrived, he showed Clint his identification.

"Frank Nolan," the man said. He was gray-haired and although he was tall, his girth made him seem shorter than he really was. It wasn't until you were standing right next to him that you realized he was well over six feet tall.

"Lieutenant Nolan," Clint said.

Dorn was lying on the floor on his back, his gun just inches from his outstretched hand. Off to one side Ted Grant was sitting at a table, holding his head in his hand. When he agreed to let Clint Adams into the saloon for a beer he hadn't expected *this*.

"A little early to open the saloon, isn't it?" Nolan asked.

Grant looked up and said, "Uh, it really isn't open, Lieutenant."

"Mr. Grant just let me in for a beer," Clint said.

"Ah, I see," Nolan said.

"You, uh, don't want one, do you?"

"No," Nolan said, "thanks. I was just talking to the two officers about the killing this morning when the report of *this* one came in. Is it a

21

coincidence that both involve you, Mr. Adams?"

"Well," Clint said, "the *first* one was a coincidence. This one, though, was not."

"Oh? How so?"

"This man seemed to think that the dead man from this morning had given me something," Clint said.

"Given you what?"

"A map, I think he said."

"A map of what?"

"That I don't know," Clint said. "All he said was that he wanted the map."

"And he didn't say what this map was a map of?" Nolan asked.

"No."

"And you don't know."

"That's right."

Grant looked up from the table again and stared at Clint. Clint hoped that Grant wouldn't mention the piece of paper Clint had asked him to put in his safe before the lieutenant arrived.

"Would, uh, you gentlemen like to talk in my office?" Grant asked.

"No," Nolan said, without looking at Grant, "this is fine."

"You, uh, don't need me, do you?"

"No," Nolan said, "you can go."

Grant stood up, then looked down at the body.

"Will you, uh, have him out of here in time for me to open—I mean, for real?"

"Sure," Nolan said, "he'll be gone. When my men get here just send them in, will you?"

"Sure. Thank you, Lieutenant."

Grant left the saloon and Clint said, "Should we sit, Lieutenant?"

"Why not? Might as well get comfortable."

They sat at the table Ted Grant had just vacated.

"All right, Mr. Adams," Nolan said, "why don't we start with what happened this morning—er, *earlier* this morning, that is."

So Clint went through it again, as he had with the bogus Lieutenant Gates.

"And the man gave you nothing?"

"No."

"And said nothing?"

"He only asked me to help him."

"Which you'd already tried to do."

"Yes," Clint said, "without much success."

"Can't blame yourself for that, Mr. Adams," Nolan said. "You did more than most people would have done."

Clint didn't reply to that.

"All right," Nolan said, "and what happened here?"

"This man came in here and introduced himself as Lieutenant Jack Gates."

"There is no Lieutenant Jack Gates," Nolan said.

"I figured that out," Clint said. "When I offered him a beer he took it, and then threw it in my face. The next thing I knew he was pointing a gun at me."

"And you killed him."

"Yes."

"Impressive."

"Not really."

"Oh, yes," Nolan said, "quite impressive. You see, Mr. Adams, I know who you are."

"Do you?"

"Yes," Nolan said. "I doubt, however, that this man did, or he would have been much more careful."

"I suppose."

At that point three uniformed policemen entered the saloon, and one of them approached Lieutenant Nolan for instructions.

"Get that body out of here," Nolan said.

"Yes, sir."

Clint and Nolan watched in silence as two of the men lifted the body and carried it out. The other man hurried out ahead of them, supposedly to clear the way.

"I hope they're not going to carry it out right through the main lobby," Clint said, "Poor Ted Grant will have a fit."

"They'll use the back way," Nolan assured him, and stood up.

"Well, Mr. Adams, with no one to back up your story—or dispute it—I guess I'm forced to accept your version as the truth."

"Thanks—I think," Clint said. "You don't have to sound so . . . dubious."

"I'm sorry," Nolan said. "Sometimes it's just the nature of my business that makes me sound that way. Certainly . . . you'd know something about that. As I understand, you were a lawman . . . once."

"A long time ago," Clint said, "yes—but I do know what you mean."

"You said there were three men this morning?" Nolan asked.

"That's right."

"Do you think this was one of them?"

"I believe he was," Clint said. "There was something familiar about him."

"Do you intend to stay in Sacramento much longer?" Nolan asked.

"I did," Clint said, "yes."

"If you do," Nolan said, "I'd advise caution. The other two might think you have this map as well."

"I'm sure they do," Clint said. "I'm only sorry I

can't convince them that I don't."

"Don't be sorry," Nolan said, moving towards the door. "You might still get the chance to try."

SEVEN

Carl Hamm watched the police carry Sam Dorn's body down an alley from the back of the hotel and toss it into the back of a buckboard. As the buckboard pulled away he ran back to the small cafe several blocks away where Ken Hill was waiting over a cup of coffee.

"So?"

"So they just carted Dorn out of there like a sack of potatoes," Hamm said, sitting across from Hill. "Christ, I need a drink."

"Dorn's dead?" Hill asked.

"That's what I just said," Hamm replied. "Dorn's dead. Jesus, Sam was good with a gun. Who *is* this guy?"

"You don't recognize the name?" Hill asked.

"What's his name again?"

"That's your problem, Carl," Hill said. "You never listen. His name is Adams, Clint Adams."

"Adams . . . Adams . . . wait a minute, I know of a Clint Adams," Hamm said, frowning. Suddenly his eyebrows shot up and he stared at Hill. "Wait a second . . . is he *that* Clint Adams?"

"Yeah," Hill said, "he's *that* Clint Adams."

"And you sent Dorn in there after him?"

"It was a good plan, Carl," Hill said. "Dorn must

have messed it up somehow."

"I'll say he messed it up," Hamm said. "He's stone cold dead."

"We're gonna need help on this," Hill said.

"You said it."

"Two, maybe three more guns ought to do it."

"*Good* guns."

"That's gonna cost, Carl."

"If there's as much money in this as you claim," Hamm said, "it'll be worth it, won't it?"

"Yeah," Hill said, "it'll be worth it. But let's remember, we're hiring help, we're not taking on any partners."

"I know that."

"Well, just make sure your tongue doesn't slip," Hill said.

"Don't worry," Hamm said, "*my* tongue ain't gonna slip."

After Nolan had left, Clint went to Ted Grant's office. The hotel manager was sitting behind his desk working on a big snifter of brandy. His color was not good.

"Is he gone?" Grant asked.

"The lieutenant?" Clint asked. "Oh, yeah, he's gone. He just left."

"Not the lieutenant," Grant said. "The body! Is the body gone?"

"Oh, yeah," Clint said, "the body's gone too, Ted. Don't worry."

"Don't worry, he says. There's a body in the middle of my saloon floor and he says I shouldn't worry. Jesus." The man looked stricken. "Is there blood on the floor?"

"A man was shot, Ted," Clint said. "Of course there's blood on the floor."

"I've got to get somebody to clean it," Grant

said. He came out of his chair, leaving the brandy snifter on the desk.

"Before you do that," Clint said, "how about giving me what I gave you to put in the safe?"

"Oh, yeah, that," Grant said. He went to the safe and swung the door open.

"You don't lock it?" Clint asked as the man gingerly handed him the bloody piece of paper. The blood had dried and now looked more brown than red.

"It takes too long to work the stupid combination," Grant said. "Besides, there's nothing of value in it. Uh, what *is* that?"

"It's a map."

"Is that what the man wanted?"

"Yes," Clint said, "but I can't for the life of me understand why."

"What is it a map of?"

"Shasta County. It shows how to get to a gold mine."

"Shasta played out long ago," Grant said. "The Chinese got whatever was left there."

"I know that."

"So why would somebody want to kill you for that map?" Grant asked.

"That's what I have to find out, Ted," Clint said.

"But—"

"Don't you have to get somebody to clean the blood off the floor in the saloon?"

"Jesus, yeah!" Grant said. "I forgot."

They left the office together, and Grant ran off to get someone to clean the floor.

Clint went back to his room with the map to examine it further. No matter how he looked at it, it didn't change. It was *still* a map of the played-out Shasta County mountains. *What* was up there that was worth killing over? Could it be that there was *still* gold up there?

Nah, there couldn't be.

He refolded the map and looked for a place to hide it. No, it wouldn't do to hide it *anywhere* in his own room. He had to find someplace else to put it, someone else to leave it with.

He folded it up, tucked it into his pocket, and left the room and the hotel.

EIGHT

Clint had to knock on Patsy's door four times before she finally opened the door. She was wearing a robe, holding it closed in the front with one hand while leaning on the open door with the other. Her eyes were barely open as she looked at him.

"Clint?"

"I'm sorry to wake you, Patsy," he said. "Can I come in for a minute?"

"Clint," she said, "I'm *really* tired. I mean, after last night . . ."

He laughed and said, "I only need a minute, Pat. Really."

"Okay," she said, "but I think you're overestimating yourself. Come on in."

She walked away from the door and sat on her bed, her shoulders slumped. He entered and closed the door behind him.

"I need you to hold onto something for me," he said to her.

"What?"

He sat on the bed next to her and handed her the stained map. "This."

She took it in her hand and asked, "What's all over it?"

"That's dry blood."

She turned her head slowly and looked at him. "What?"

"Dry . . . blood."

"Eek," she said, and dropped the map to the floor.

Clint picked it up and said, "A man died over this this morning."

"What are you talking about?"

He told her the whole story, including the attempt on his life in the hotel saloon that morning.

"You've been busy," she said.

"I didn't go looking for this, believe me," he said. "But now that I have it, I have to figure out what to do with it."

"Why not just give it to the police?"

"That's a good question," he said.

"And," she said, "do you have a good answer?"

"No, I don't," he said. "I just feel like I should hold onto it for a little while. I mean, the little guy was so *desperate* for me to keep it from the wrong hands."

"But if it's worthless, like you say . . ."

"That's what I have to find out," Clint said, "whether it *is* worthless or not."

"How are you gonna do that?"

"I don't know," he said, "short of actually going up there and *using* the damned thing."

"You might be wasting a trip."

"I know," he said. "There's got to be somebody I can talk to about Shasta." He held the map out to her and said, "Will you keep this for me?"

"What if they come after me for it?"

"Don't worry," he said. "Nobody will know you have it. I made sure I wasn't followed."

"Oh, all right," she said. "Put it somewhere."

He looked around, then decided to just put it under her mattress.

"Great place," she said.

He kissed her on the cheek and said, "Thanks, Patsy."

"When will you be back?" she asked.

"Later," he said. "Go back to sleep and don't think about it anymore."

"Sure," she said, as he went out the door. "He puts a bloodstained map underneath my bed—the blood of a *dead* man—and tells me not to think about it."

She sat there for a few moments, then said, "Oh, the hell with it."

She lay down and went to sleep.

NINE

Clint went back to his hotel and once again sought out Ted Grant. This time Grant was in the saloon, supervising the scrubbing of the floor.

"Is it coming out?" Clint asked.

"Yes, thank God," Grant said. "We'll be able to open on time."

"Good," Clint said. "I'd hate to think that I had ruined your business."

"Don't worry," Grant said. "I wouldn't have held you responsible."

"That's a comfort. Ted, tell me something."

"What?"

"Do you know anyone who's knowledgeable about the Gold Rush? About mines in general—maybe about Shasta County in particular?"

"No, no," Grant said, "and no."

"But you knew Shasta was played out."

"*All* the mines in northern California are played out," Grant said. "Everybody knows that."

"You'd think so, wouldn't you?"

"Sorry I can't help you," Grant said. "Get that spot over there!"

"Thanks anyway," Clint said, but Grant wasn't hearing him anymore.

Clint needed someone else who lived in Sacra-

33

mento, had lived there a while, and might know somebody with the information he needed.

He left the hotel and headed back down towards the docks, where this whole thing had started that morning.

When he walked into the Cafe Adventure Eddie Maples rubbed his eyes, as if he couldn't believe it.

"You can't be here for lunch," Maple said, "so you must have come back for your breakfast."

"Actually," Clint said, "I came for some information. Do you have time to talk?"

"As you can see," Maple said, indicating his empty tables, "I'm all filled up—but let them wait. Come, I'll get you a beer."

Clint agreed to the beer. He didn't see how Eddie and Estelle could ruin *that*.

Each armed with a beer, they sat at the nearest table.

"What can I do for you?" Maple asked.

Clint explained what he needed.

"Does this have to do with what happened this morning?" Maple wanted to know.

"I really would rather not say, Eddie," Clint said. "If you can't help me, I'll understand." He started to get up from the table.

"No, no," Maple said, waving him back down into his seat. "I didn't say I *couldn't* help you, did I? Sit back down."

Clint sat.

"I know a man," Maple said. "He eats in here a lot—*lunch* and *dinner*. Unlike you, he likes *everything* Estelle cooks."

"You never told her I didn't like her cooking, did you?" Clint asked.

"Of course not," Maple said. "I told her you had

someplace else that you'd rather go."

"Eddie . . ."

"No," Eddie said, "I'm kidding. I didn't tell her that either. I told her you never had the time to come here for anything but breakfast."

"If she sees me here now she'll make me eat something," Clint said.

"Don't worry," he said, "she's out shopping. You'll be gone before she gets back."

"Okay," Clint said, "what about this fella you know."

"He's lived here for years, but he spent some time mining gold—maybe even up around Shasta. He should be able to tell you what you want to know."

"Who is he?"

"His name's Ben Schutz," Maple said. "He's a big fella, big through the chest and arms and shoulders, you know? Probably from all that mining, lifting heavy rocks and such. Hell, he may have even worked on ships at one time, who knows? For a relatively young fella, he's done a lot."

"Maybe he just bulked up that way eating your food," Clint said.

"Don't laugh," Maple said. "That might even be it."

"Can I have his address, or do I have to sit here and wait for him to come in?"

"He don't come in every day," Maple said, "or you *could* wait. He lives at the Carlyle Hotel. You know where that is?"

Clint thought a moment, then said, "Yeah, I do. He lives there?"

"They rent him a room by the month. He's been there for years."

The Carlyle was about halfway between Clint's hotel and the docks, not far from Sacramento's

Chinatown. Not in the best of neighborhoods, but certainly not in the worst.

"Thanks, Eddie," Clint said. "I'll look him up right away."

"In a hurry, are you?"

"No," Clint said, standing up, "but I know some other fellas who might be."

TEN

Clint walked to the Carlyle Hotel, taking a route that took him through Chinatown. According to Maple, it was shorter that way.

When he reached the Carlyle he presented himself at the front desk and asked for Ben Schutz.

"Who wants him?" the bored-looking man asked. He certainly hadn't gotten the job because of his manners, a fact that Clint pointed out to him.

The man smiled and said, "I don't got to have any manners. I own the place."

"Well, Eddie Maple sent me over to talk to Ben Schutz," Clint said.

"You a friend of Eddie's?"

"That's right."

"Well, why didn't you say so in the first place," the man said. "My name's Jerry Bates. Ben's room is at the top of the stairs, first door on your left."

"Thanks."

Clint went up the stairs and knocked on Ben Schutz's door.

"Who is it?"

"My name's Clint Adams," Clint called out. "Eddie Maple sent me."

He heard heavy footsteps, and then the door swung open. Maple hadn't been kidding about

Schutz's size. He was almost swollen with muscle through the chest, shoulders, and upper arms. His strength must have been impressive—a fact Clint hoped he'd never have to test.

"Clint Adams, you said?" Schutz asked.

"That's right."

"You the fella they call the Gunsmith?"

"Yes."

"Come on in," Schutz said. "Maple mentioned to me that you were in town."

"Is that right?" Clint asked. He stepped into the room and closed the door behind him. "Who else did he tell I was in town?"

"Nobody," Schutz said. "Eddie and me, we got an information system. He tells me things I don't know, I tell him things he don't know, and then we *both* know what's goin' on."

"Sounds like it works."

"It does," Schutz said.

The room seemed small, which may have been due in part to Schutz's size. He also seemed to have a lot of things in the room besides the bed and the dresser it had come with. He had a big, comfortable-looking armchair, which he now sank into.

"Found this in the street, where somebody tossed it," Schutz said, slapping the arms. "Fixed it up myself and kept it. It's comfortable."

"It looks comfortable."

"Sorry I don't have anything for you to sit on but the bed."

"That's fine."

"Eddie tell you what I do?"

"No."

"I run an information service," Schutz said. "I know everything."

"Everything?"

"What I don't know," the man said, "ain't worth knowing."

Schutz looked to be in his early forties, with a bushy brown mustache and sharp, intelligent eyes behind a pair of eyeglasses.

"I assume you're here because you want to know something."

"That's right."

"Let's have it then," Schutz said. He leaned his head back against the cushion of the chair, made himself comfortable, and closed his eyes.

"I'm interested in gold mining in Shasta County," Clint said.

"Shasta's played out," Schutz said.

"I know that," Clint said. Then he added, "I *thought* I knew that. Since this morning a man's been killed over a map, and an attempt was made on my life over the same map."

Schutz opened his eyes and stared at Clint. He looked suddenly *very* interested. "Do you have the map?"

Clint hesitated, and Schutz held up his hand.

"Okay, do you have it *with* you so I can look at it?" Schutz asked.

"No."

"Can you get it?"

"If I have to," Clint said, "I guess I could get it. Why?"

"Because I'd know more if I could see it, that's why," Schutz said.

"What does it matter?" Clint asked. "I thought Shasta was played out."

"It is," Schutz said, and then added, "Mostly."

"What does *mostly* mean?"

"I did some mining up in Shasta a long time ago," Schutz said.

"How did you do?"

"Took out my fair share of dust," Schutz said. "No nuggets, but some dust. Not enough to make me rich, but enough to keep me happy for a while. While I was up there I heard talk about a section that was untouched, only nobody knew where it was. Some folks thought that's all it was, talk."

"And what do *you* think, Mr. Schutz?"

"First of all, I think you should call me Ben, Clint," Schutz said.

"All right," Clint said. "What do you think, Ben? *Was* it all talk?"

"I have an open mind," Schutz said. "I'd like to see that map, though."

Clint hesitated.

"If Eddie sent you to me," Schutz said, "he must have vouched for me."

"He did."

"Well, then, you're either gonna talk to me or you're not," Schutz said. "If you're not, then we don't have anything to say to each other anymore, do we? I mean, *you* came to *me*, right?"

"All right," Clint said after a moment. "I can get the map."

"Get it then," Schutz said, "and bring it here. I'll tell you if it's any good or not."

"Just by looking at it?"

"Yep, that's right," Schutz said, "just by looking at it."

ELEVEN

Clint was fairly sure that he had not been followed, either to Eddie Maple's Cafe Adventure or to the Hotel Carlyle. He was also *very* sure that he had not been followed to Patsy Kelly's. What he couldn't be sure of, of course, was who might be waiting for him at his hotel now, either to make another attempt on his life or to simply start following him.

As he approached his hotel he tried to study the street without seeming to. If he *did* manage to spot someone watching him, he didn't want them to know they *had* been spotted.

He did the same as he entered the hotel. He studied the lobby, taking his time walking through it to the dining room. From the dining room he went to the saloon.

The saloon was fairly busy, as it was approaching late afternoon. Half the tables were occupied, and there were a few places left at the bar. Clint fitted himself into one of the places and ordered a beer from the bartender, Harry Bosco.

"I heard what happened in here today," Bosco said, placing the beer in front of Clint.

"Yeah," Clint said, "a little bit of excitement."

"What was the guy after?"

"Me, I guess," Clint said.

"That reputation, huh?" Bosco said, nodding knowingly. "It's a magnet for trouble, all right. Guess that's somethin' you gotta learn to live with, huh?"

"I guess," Clint said.

He was saved from having to talk about it further when Bosco had to move down the bar to serve someone else. Harry Bosco was one of the most talkative bartenders Clint had ever met, and he had met hundreds, maybe *thousands* of bartenders over the years. He was a nice enough man, but after a while you just wanted him to be quiet, go away, and talk to somebody else.

Clint decided to take his beer to a table before Bosco could come back. His intention was to nurse the beer for a while, and then go over to the restaurant where Patsy worked for dinner. He hoped that Patsy would leave the map in her room and not carry it on her. Actually, the dry blood would probably keep her from touching it at all.

Clint sipped his beer and studied the room. There was a poker game starting at one table, a game he had played in a few times over the past week. Maybe later he'd even join in again.

Most of the men in the room were recognizable as regulars or semi-regulars. There were very few faces that Clint didn't think he had seen before.

He knew he was involved in an exercise in futility. In a fairly crowded saloon—which was becoming more crowded by the moment—it was almost impossible to spot someone who might be watching you, unless his manner was decidedly obvious. All Clint was doing was giving himself eyestrain, and there was always the possibility that someone might catch Clint looking at him, and think *he* was watching *him*. In a roomful of men who were drinking, it didn't take much to get someone mad at you. He finally decided to finish the beer and walk over to the restaurant for an early dinner. The incident that morning had destroyed his usual breakfast-lunch-dinner schedule, and he found that he was ravenously hungry.

"We should be watching Adams even now," Carl Hamm said, "instead of sitting here. What if he decides to leave Sacramento with the map?"

"He won't," Ken Hill said.

"Why do you think that?"

"Because it'll take him a while to decide that the map is real," Hill said.

"Why?"

"Because everybody knows that Shasta County is played out."

"*We* don't know that, do we?" Hamm asked.

"No," Hill said, "the fact is, *we* know *better* than that."

"So then what's gonna make him think it's real?" Hamm asked.

"Well," Hill said, "we probably did a lot to help him decide it's real by sending Dorn after him."

"*You* sent Dorn after him," Hamm said.

"I know," Hill said, "and it might have been a mistake."

"It was a mistake for Dorn," Hamm said.

Hill gave Hamm a baleful look and said, "Right, Carl. I realize that. That's why we're here in this pisspot of a saloon waiting to hire some help."

Hamm looked around the small, ill-smelling saloon, The Bloody Bucket, and asked, "What kind of help are we gonna find here, Ken?"

"This is a lousy place to drink, Carl," Hill said,

"but it's a good place to hire some reliable help. Believe me, all we got to do is sit here a while and wait."

Hamm stared down at the warm beer that had been served to him in a dirty glass and said, "I could wait better if I had a decent glass of beer."

"Stop complaining," Hill said. "At least there's nothing dead floating in it."

TWELVE

The restaurant Patsy Kelly worked in was called Babe's Restaurant. Babe, Patsy said, was a forty-four-year-old man who weighed over three hundred pounds and *never* came out of the kitchen to meet any of his customers. He was a good cook, as evidenced by the fact—she said—that he ate more of his cooking than anyone, and when people wanted to compliment him on his cooking they sent a message back to him with Patsy. She had been working for him for three years, and she had *never* seen him come out of the kitchen to meet any of his customers.

When Clint walked into Babe's, Patsy was carrying a tray in each hand. Babe's was small, and from early afternoon to late evening it was the busiest place in Sacramento. Babe—Patsy said—hated to pay for help, so he had to find a waitress who would work for him knowing that she was going to do *all* the work. He had gone through dozens of waitresses before he'd finally hired Patsy. She was the only waitress he'd ever had who could handle the pressure of serving people quickly and getting them out so that there was an open table for the next diner.

Clint had rarely had trouble finding a table since

45

he'd started eating at Babe's because he dined alone. Most of the other tables were taken up by two, three, and four diners at a time. As he got to the door he had to step aside to allow a man to leave, and so when he entered he saw that there was an open table against the wall. Although it hadn't been cleaned off yet, he went over and sat down.

Patsy delivered her two trays of food, and then hurried over to clean his table off.

"The usual?" she asked.

"Yes," he said. He usually ordered Babe's beef stew, because it was easier than making Patsy wait while he decided what he wanted to eat.

"Comin' up," she said, and hurried off.

The first time he had eaten in Babe's he had watched Patsy work, never breaking stride, never dropping a dish or so much as spilling a drop of water or coffee, and he had admired her. He had eaten there three times before he came back one night as Babe's was closing, and although they hadn't spoken a word beyond his ordering his dinner, she'd turned to him and said, "I was afraid you weren't coming."

"You were expecting me?"

"After the first night," she'd said. "After *three* nights I had just about given up on you."

They had gone to his hotel room that night, made love, and then talked and made love all night long. Since then they had spent almost every night together.

When she came out of the kitchen she was carrying his dinner, a basket of rolls, and a mug of beer. She hurried to his table and served him with a quick, "Enjoy. We'll talk later."

There was usually a bit of a lull between late lunch and early dinner, and it would soon be upon them. It only lasted for about twenty minutes or so, but that would be enough for them to say what they had to say.

He ate slowly, enjoying each bite, soaking up the gravy with the fresh rolls and nursing his beer so he wouldn't have to ask her for another. As it turned out he didn't have to ask because she brought him another before he was half finished.

He watched as people finished eating and left faster than people were coming in, and before long the lull was upon them. In Babe's a lull meant that only half of the tables were full.

She came over to him and brushed a lock of auburn hair from her forehead.

"This is crazy," he said. "You can't keep up this pace."

"Why not?" she asked. "I'm young and healthy, and besides, it makes the day go faster. Before I know it," she added, leaning over so he could only hear her, "I'm in bed with you."

"Lucky me," he said, and meant it.

According to Patsy—and he had no reason to disbelieve her—in the three years she had worked there she had *never* gone home with a customer, until he'd walked in.

"As soon as you walked through the door," she had told him, "I knew you'd be the one." Not that she had ever *planned* on going home with someone. "Even if we had met in the street," she'd told him, "you would have been the one."

"What made me so lucky?" he'd asked.

She had smiled and said, "Damned if I know."

"Ready for coffee?" she asked now.

"In a minute," he said. "I need to talk to you about that . . . thing I gave you."

"That *thing* is still where you put it," she said. She put her hand in her apron pocket and came out with a key, which she placed on the table. "There's my key. You can go pick it up yourself, because I ain't *touchin'* it."

"Can't say I blame you," he said. He took the key and pocketed it. "I'll have that coffee now."

"Comin' up," she said. She turned away, then turned back and said, "If you need me to hold that . . . thing for you again, just let me know. All right?"

"All right, Patsy," he said. "Thanks."

She smiled and went to the kitchen to get him his coffee.

THIRTEEN

After his early dinner Clint left Babe's, which was once again in full swing. Patsy did not even have time to wave to him as he left.

Stepping out into the street, he looked around and determined to his satisfaction that he was not being followed. Still, he walked away aimlessly, keeping an eye behind him, to make absolutely certain that he was not being trailed. The last thing he wanted to do was put Patsy in danger by leading someone to her home.

Finally, he made for her place and let himself in with his key. The bed was unmade, and the place was in a general state of disarray. If he had not known that it *always* looked like that, he would have thought that her place had been searched.

He went to the bed, lifted the mattress, and took out the brown-stained map. Some of the dry blood had flaked off, and he wiped it away before lowering the mattress again.

He sat on the bed and once again—it seemed like for the *hundredth* time—he examined the map. It didn't mean anything to him at that moment, and probably wouldn't until he was actually *in* Shasta County, with the map in front of him.

He folded the map and put it in his shirt pocket.

He walked to the window and looked outside at the alley below. Patsy's room was on the second floor above a general store, and the only window she had overlooked the alley below, which was empty.

Clint almost felt as if he was on the run, constantly watching his backtrail for sign of a posse— and perhaps, in a way, he *was* on the run. There were at least two men out there who wanted what he had in his pocket, and they were probably not ready to give up just yet. He could *still* save himself some trouble by turning the damned thing over to Lieutenant Frank Nolan, but he wasn't yet prepared to do that.

He left Patsy's place and went downstairs to find himself a horse-drawn cab. He'd take *that* to within walking distance of Ben Schutz's hotel, and then would walk the rest of the way. Again, he was just playing it safe and making sure that he wasn't followed to Schutz's place. Schutz was just as innocent a bystander in this as Patsy was, and he didn't want to put the man's life in danger either.

On the street the map seemed to be burning a hole in his chest.

FOURTEEN

Clint took twice as long to get to Ben Schutz's hotel as he might have, but once he was there he was certain no one had come with him. Jesus, he thought, he could *never* live as a hunted fugitive. He didn't think his nerves would be able to take it.

"Back again?" the owner and desk clerk, Jerry, asked.

"Yes," Clint said. "Is he up there?"

"He's most always up there," Jerry said. "Often takes his *meals* up there. They're brought over from the Cafe Adventure. The only time he leaves is to go *there* and eat."

"Interesting," Clint said, and went up the steps.

He wondered how Ben Schutz managed to get all of his information if he hardly ever left his hotel room.

He knocked on the door.

"Who is it?"

"Clint Adams again."

Once again the heavy footsteps—he could *feel* them as well as hear them—and the door swung open.

"Come on in," Schutz said, moving away from the door.

Clint entered and closed the door behind him. When he turned, Schutz was settled into his armchair, just as he had been when Clint left. It was as if he had never moved.

"Did you bring it?" Schutz asked.

"I brought it," Clint said.

He took it out of his pocket, handed it to Schutz, and then sat down on the bed. He marveled at how neat the room looked when compared to Patsy's, even though Schutz had a lot more in it. For one thing the bed was perfectly made, and did not even reveal the fact that Clint had been sitting on it earlier.

He watched as Schutz opened the map, totally ignoring the fact that it was crusted with a dead man's blood. Schutz leaned forward in his chair as he examined it. It grew so quiet in the room that Clint thought he could actually *hear* the silence!

He waited as long as he could and then said, "Well?"

Schutz looked at him briefly, and then back at the map in his hands.

"I'll tell you the truth," he said. "I always thought the talk of an untouched mine was nonsense."

"And now?"

"And now . . . if this map is genuine . . . I believe it might actually exist." He held the map up so Clint could see it. "And I believe this might lead us right to it."

Clint waited a moment, and then said, "Us?"

"That is," Schutz said, "unless you want to try to find it yourself. Have you ever been to Shasta County?"

"No . . ."

"You *might* find the mine on your own," Schutz went on, "but if what you tell me is true, you might also have some company on your tail. You could use another hand."

"Wait a minute," Clint said. "I haven't said anything about actually going up there."

"Hey," Schutz said, "that's fine with me. I'll buy
the map off of you."

"Buy it?"

"How much do you want?"

"I don't know. I haven't even thought—"

"I'll give you a thousand dollars."

"A thousand?"

"All right," Schutz said, "*two* thousand."

"Ben, I don't know if—"

"Twenty-five hundred dollars."

Schutz got up out of his chair and knelt by his
bed. From underneath it he took a metal strongbox, which he opened with a key. He took three
stacks of money out of the box and tossed them
on the bed.

"There's a thousand dollars in each stack," he
said. "I'll give you three thousand."

"Hold on a second," Clint said, holding up his
hand.

"You want more?"

"I don't even want to *talk* about selling it," Clint
said. "I haven't made up my mind *what* I want to
do with it—if anything."

Schutz stood up, leaving the money on the bed
with the open strongbox.

"You're going to have to make up your mind,
Clint," Schutz said. "There are men out there who
have already killed once for it, and tried to kill *you*
once. They're not about to give up. *They* obviously think that the map is real."

"So do you."

"I'm not convinced."

"But you offered me three thousand dollars for
it," Clint said.

Schutz spread his hands and said, "I've been in this room a long time, Clint. I could use a trip to the Shasta Mountains. *This*," he said, pointing to the map, "if it's real, gives me a reason to go."

"You mean you'd go all that way just on the off chance it's real?"

"Hey," Schutz said, "it's really not *all* that way, and it's something to do."

Schutz was still holding the map. He took a step towards Clint and held it out to him.

"It's up to you," he said as Clint accepted the map back. "You can either sell the map to me, or we can make the trip together. Your decision."

Clint refolded the map and stuck it in his pocket.

"Or," Schutz said, "you can burn the damned thing."

Clint gave Schutz a sharp look. "What would that accomplish?"

"Probably nothing," Schutz said. "Your life would probably *still* be in danger."

"And if we go together," Clint said, "*your* life will be in danger too."

"My life hasn't been in danger for quite a while," he said. "In fact, my life hasn't even been *interesting* for a while. It would make for a pretty nice change, don't you think?"

"I can think of *better* ways of changing it," Clint said frankly.

"Maybe," Schutz said, and for the first time since he'd met the man Clint noticed that the man's eyes were actually shining. "But nothing else would have quite the *bite* that this does."

Clint stood up and said, "I'm going to have to give this some thought, Ben."

Schutz spread his hands again and said, "I'll be here, Clint."

Clint nodded and started for the door.

"Oh," Schutz said, "by the way, you can trust me not to say anything to anyone about this."

Clint opened the door, turned, and said, "I wasn't worried about that."

FIFTEEN

Ken Hill paid the three men half their money, and he and Carl Hamm watched as they walked out the door.

"We waited here all that time for *them*?" Hamm asked Hill.

"Well, I had to rely on someone else to alert me when someone reliable walked in," Hill said.

"And who was that?" Hamm asked.

"The bartender."

Hamm looked over at the bartender, who looked more like he belonged in front of the bar than behind it.

"*He* told you these three were reliable?"

"That's right," Hill said.

"Well, for a hundred bucks apiece they better be," Hamm said. "When are they supposed to do it?"

"Tonight," Hill said. "They'll either get the map from Clint Adams or kill him."

"Or get killed," Hamm said.

"Don't be ridiculous," Hill said. "There are three of them."

"You're the one who pointed out to *me* who he is, remember?" Hamm said.

"He's still only one man, Carl," Hill said. "No,

I don't think we'll have anything to worry about after tonight."

"And we won't have a map either," Hamm pointed out. "What if they kill him and don't come up with the map?"

"I remember enough of the map to get us to the gold," Hill said.

"Then why are we botherin' about the damned map?" Hamm wanted to know.

"Because we don't want anyone *else* beating us there, that's why," Hill said. "Hell, we don't even want anyone else *knowin'* about it. That's why the little man Smith had to be killed, and that's why Clint Adams has to die—Gunsmith or *no* Gunsmith."

"Well, when do we leave then?" Hamm said. "If we're gonna get that gold I'd like to get to it."

"As soon as we have that map, or know that Adams is dead, we'll leave," Hill said. "With a little luck that should be tomorrow."

"So what do we do until then?"

"I don't know about you," Hill said, "but since we'll be in the mountains for a while, I'm gonna go and get me a woman and have a night that will hold me."

"That don't sound like a bad idea," Hamm said, and both men started to get up.

"Hey, Hill."

"What?"

"What if Adams has already shown the map to someone else?"

Hill made a face and said, "What the hell did you have to go and say that for?"

"I don't know," Hamm said with a shrug. "It was just a thought."

"Yeah, well," Hill said, "it's a thought I'd rather not have. I'm tellin' you now. Once we're up there

at the mine, if *anybody* comes near it I'm blowin'
them from here right straight to Hell. I ain't about
to share that gold with *nobody* else!"

As Hill stormed out of The Bloody Bucket, Hamm
had an uncomfortable thought.

What if that meant *him* too?

Cheap labor.

That was the first thought that came to Clint
Adams's mind when he saw the three men.

He was walking down the street towards his
hotel and saw two of them first. They were across
the street, and they were making no pretense about
what they were doing. When they saw him they
came to attention and *looked* across the street
towards the hotel. That was when he saw the
third man, positioned right outside the hotel.

Clint stopped to study the situation for a moment. The longer he looked the more convinced
he was that there were only those three, which
meant that the situation *could* have been a whole
lot worse.

Of course, the situation was *far* from being good,
but unless they had somebody positioned at a window, or on a roof, with a rifle, then he only had to
worry about these three.

As he started walking towards the hotel again,
the thought of turning and running never entered
his mind.

SIXTEEN

As Clint approached the front of the hotel, the two men across the way started across the street, while the third man simply stood his ground. They were all armed, and they all looked like they thought they could scare anybody with just a look. It was Clint's guess that they had been doing just that for a long time and no one had yet proven that they *couldn't*.

"Are you Clint Adams?"

It would have been just as easy to say no, but instead Clint said, "That's right. Can I help you gents with something?"

The spokesman was apparently the man who had been waiting in front of the hotel. The other two men remained in the street, with about five feet between them.

"You got something that belongs to a friend of ours," the spokesman said. He had a scar above his right eye from a wound that hadn't healed well. Clint started to think of him as Scar Face.

"A friend of yours?" Clint asked. "My guess is somebody's paying you boys for this little visit. Well, I got news for you. Whatever you're being paid, it isn't enough to die over. Take my advice and go on home."

Scar Face looked at the other three men, and they shared a chuckle.

"That's tough talk for one man facing three," Scar Face said then.

"No, it's not," Clint said, "and I'll tell you why." He indicated all three men with a wave of his finger and said, "It's my opinion that any three men who feel they have to face one man together—well, those three men aren't *really* men, are they?"

"Oh, no?" one of the men in the street asked. He had ears like jug handles, and that was how Clint thought of him. "Then what are they?"

"Well, since you asked," Clint said, "I'd call those three men cowards."

"Why you—" Jug Ears started.

"Easy, Reese," Scar Face said. "He's tryin' to rile you . . . ain't ya, mister?"

"No," Clint said. "I'm just telling you three what I think of you. I'll make this real easy for you boys. There's nothing I have that I'll hand over to you, so whatever else you want here, you better get to it."

"Why should you care about it?" the third man asked. Clint dubbed him Needle Nose because he had a nose that came to a point. "From what I hear it's just a piece of paper you got. Give it up and go on livin'. That ain't much of a decision, is it?"

"I'll give you fellas a decision to make," Clint said. "Walk away now and go on living."

Scar Face looked at his friends, Jug Ears and Needle Nose, and shook his head. "It don't sound like this fella is too smart, fellas," he said. "I guess we got to do what we got to do."

Clint didn't wait for them to decide what they had to do. He took three quick steps to put him face to face with Scar Face.

"Wha—" the man said, but before he could react Clint had snatched his gun from his holster and pistol-whipped him across the face with it. A gash opened on his cheek, and Clint knew he'd have another scar—if he lived long enough for the wound to heal.

With Scar Face's gun in his hand he turned on the other two men, who were caught by surprise by his action. He covered them with the gun.

"Back off," Clint said. "Walk away and live. I'm giving you the same choice again. I won't offer it a third time."

"What about *him*?" Needle Nose asked, indicating Scar Face, who was down on one knee with both hands over his face.

"Pick him up and take him with you."

He backed off so the two men could mount the boardwalk and pick up Scar Face. Supporting him between them, they started across the street.

Clint watched them until they reached the other side, and then turned to go back inside. He was alerted by a wild scream, and then turned to see Scar Face rushing across the street towards him. He had apparently grabbed a gun from one of the other men, and he was cursing angrily at Clint as he ran.

Clint had no time to shout a warning. He raised the gun he had taken from the man and fired just an instant before Scar Face would have. The bullet struck Scar Face in the chest, stopping him in his tracks. He stood stock still for a moment, then took one step and fell onto his face. Clint quickly looked towards the other two men.

"What about you two?" he asked.

"Hey!" Jug Ears said, raising his hands. "We're goin'." His holster was empty, so it was his gun Scar Face had snatched. Jug Ears seemed content,

though, to walk away and leave his gun in the
street with the dead man.

Clint turned as people came out of the hotel, Ted
Grant among them.

"What happened?" Grant asked.

"At least I didn't get blood on your floor this
time, Ted," Clint said. "You better send for the
police."

SEVENTEEN

Lieutenant Frank Nolan was not a happy man.

"I've had more killings and shootings in the past two days than I had the previous month, Mr. Adams. Why do you suppose that is?"

"Well," Clint said, "if I was in your shoes, I'd have to figure that it had something to do with me."

"Correct."

"But I'd be wrong—that is, *you'd* be wrong, Lieutenant," Clint said.

"Oh? And why is that?"

"Because I'm not the one who went looking for this," Clint said, "either time."

"No," Nolan said, "I'll have to admit that *it* seems to have come looking for *you*—but it all still becomes my problem, doesn't it?"

"I suppose so," Clint said. "I'm really sorry you have to clean up this mess again, Lieutenant."

Nolan looked out the door of the hotel from the lobby, where he and Clint were talking, and watched as his men lifted the body and carried it away.

Ted Grant was also in the lobby, wringing his hands and looking worried. "This is not gonna be good for business," he said.

Nolan looked at Grant and said, "And *my* business is too good. You know, we'd both be a lot better off if your friend left town."

"And took my trouble with me?" Clint said.

"That's the way it would happen," Nolan said.

"But then you'd never find out who killed that fella Smith, and who's been trying to kill me."

Nolan gave Clint a humorless smile and said, "I'd risk it."

"Well, before I leave, can you tell me who that fella out there was?" Clint asked.

"Sure," Nolan said. "Cheap labor named Calvin Dolan. Usually worked with a couple of other beauties named Collins and Reese."

"Yeah," Clint said, "he called one of the other fellas Reese."

"Big jug-handle ears?" Nolan asked.

"That's the guy," Clint said, "and the other man had a nose that came to a point."

"That'd be Del Collins. I'll have the two of them rounded up, but if they were doin' this for money they'd have no idea what the real reason was."

"I guess not."

"But you do, don't you, Adams?" Nolan asked. "Only for some reason you're not talking. This couldn't be something personal with you, could it? Something you want to take care of yourself?"

"I don't know these fellas, Lieutenant," Clint said. "If I did I would have told you."

"But what were they after, these two men you killed?" Nolan asked.

Clint was honest, up to a point. "Both fellas said that I had something they wanted. The one this morning mentioned a map. The one just now—or maybe one of his partners—mentioned a piece of paper."

"A map of what? What kind of piece of paper?"

"I didn't ask," Clint said. "I knew I didn't have anything I was going to give them, and I told them so."

Nolan looked out the door again. The body was gone. He looked back at Clint.

"I guess I should be glad you didn't kill all three of them just now," he said. "You *could* have killed all three, couldn't you?"

"Maybe," Clint said, "but I gave them a chance to walk away *without* shots being fired, Lieutenant. I didn't *want* to kill anyone."

"You could have run away when you saw them."

"What would that have accomplished?" Clint asked.

"It would have been better for business," he heard Ted Grant say under his breath.

"I guess you're right," Nolan said. "They probably would have kept on looking for you until they found you. This way one is dead, and the other two have given up. Whoever hired them, though, will hire more."

"If that's the case," Clint said, "then you're probably right, Lieutenant."

"I am?" Nolan asked. "About what?"

"Maybe it *is* time I moved on."

"Well, if you do," Nolan said, "I wish you luck."

"Thanks."

"I also wish you'd let me know for sure," Nolan said, "so I can stop holding my breath."

"I'll leave word for you, Lieutenant."

Nolan waved a hand and went out the door.

"Did you mean that?" Grant asked. "Are you gonna be leaving?"

Clint turned to Grant and put his hand on the man's shoulder. "Don't sound so hopeful, Ted."

"Clint, I didn't mean—"

"I know you didn't mean it, Ted," Clint said.

"You're just worried about business. I can understand that."

"Thanks."

"And yes," Clint said, "I think I will be leaving."

"At the risk of sounding indelicate," Ted Grant said, "when?"

EIGHTEEN

When was a question he couldn't answer. Not yet. Not until he straightened some things out with some people.

"Ted," he said, "a young lady will be here looking for me pretty soon."

"The waitress?" Grant asked. "The one with the big—"

"That's the one," Clint said. "Her name's Patsy Kelly. Let her into my room, all right?"

"Sure, Clint," Grant said, "but what should I tell her you're doing?"

"Making travel plans," Clint said, and left.

For the third time that day Clint went to the Carlyle Hotel.

"He's there," Jerry said, as he walked in. "He's eatin'."

"Thanks."

Clint knocked, and was admitted to Ben Schutz's room.

"Back already?"

"I'm ready."

"To sell?"

"To go to Shasta County," Clint said. "I'm ready to check out that mine and see if it's real."

"Why the change of heart?"

Clint told him what had been waiting for him when he got back to the White Palace Hotel.

"Looks like they're not gonna give up on you," Schutz said.

"Well," Clint said, "if they still want me they're going to have to chase me all the way to Shasta County. When can you be able to leave?"

Schutz thought a moment, and then said, "Thirty-six hours."

"All right," Clint said. "Eight A.M. Monday morning. Right?"

"Right," Schutz said. "I'll outfit us."

"We'll split the cost."

"No argument from me," Schutz said. "We'll meet right out front at eight A.M."

"I'll be there."

Schutz nodded and the two men shook hands.

"Oh," Clint said, "one more thing."

"What's that?"

"Can you shoot?"

"With a rifle, yes," Schutz said. "With a handgun I can't hit the side of a barn—from the inside."

"That'll have to do," Clint said. "See you in thirty-six hours."

When Clint got back to his hotel room Patsy was waiting there for him. She was in bed and naked, with a concerned look on her face.

"What's this about travel arrangements?" she asked as he walked in. "And I heard something about a shooting outside."

Clint sat on the bed with her, told her what had happened, and told her what was *going* to happen.

"So you're just leaving?" she asked.

"In thirty-six hours, yes," he said.

"To go hunting for gold."

"Well . . . not exactly," he said. "Yes, I'm going to go looking for a gold mine, but I don't intend to go hunting for gold. What I'm trying to do is keep from getting killed."

"You mean they'll come after you again?"

"And again, until they either kill me or get the map," he said.

"That damned map again."

"Yes."

"Why don't you throw it away?" she asked. "Before it gets stained with *your* blood too?"

"I thought about that," he said, "but in the end I decided that this was the best course of action."

"It stinks," she said.

"Patsy—"

"I knew you'd be leaving eventually," she said, "but I didn't expect it to be so . . . abrupt."

"It's not abrupt," he said. "We still have thirty-six hours."

"That's *all* we have," she complained.

"Thirty-six hours is a long time," he said.

"No, it's not."

"I guess that depends on how you look at it," he said. "Either way, let's not waste any of it. Okay?"

He put his hand beneath her chin, tilted her chin up, and kissed her. He ran his tongue along her bottom teeth, and then her tongue touched his.

"All right?" he asked again.

"Yes," she said, "oh, yes, very all right . . ."

He slid his hands beneath the sheet and cupped her breasts. They kissed again, this time longer, deeper, and she tore at his clothes so that before long they were both naked . . .

A little later Patsy said in the dark, "I have an idea."

"What?"

"I'll come with you."

Clint paused, trying to find a way to put it that wouldn't upset her.

"No," he finally decided on.

"Why not?"

"Well," he said, "for one thing it's too dangerous. I'll have people after me trying to kill me."

"So what?" she said. "I could get killed here too, crossing the street."

"What would Babe do without you?"

"He'll get along."

"I have a partner, Patsy," Clint said. "He wouldn't agree to it."

"Maybe he would," she said. "After all, I could cook—I *can* cook, you know. Maybe not as good as Babe, but probably better than you or your partner."

"Patsy . . . I can't let you come," he said.

"I'm not asking you to make it . . . permanent or anything, Clint. I mean, after you find the mine we could come back here and . . . celebrate."

"Patsy—"

"And I'm not asking for any gold or anything," she said.

"Patsy . . . I just can't take you with me. Please understand."

She went silent in the dark now, and then she snuggled up against him. He put his arm around her and she nestled her head onto his chest.

"All right," she said finally, "I understand."

NINETEEN

"So what the hell are we gonna do now?" Carl Hamm asked Ken Hill. "Or maybe I shouldn't even be askin' you that question. Maybe *I* should make some of the decisions around here from now on."

"Okay," Hill said. He sat back in his chair and folded his arms across his chest.

They were back in The Bloody Bucket, and they knew what had happened in front of the White Palace Hotel between Clint Adams and the three men they'd "hired." One of the men had actually come back—the one with the jug ears—to tell them, and had *returned* the money he and the others had been paid, except for the money that had been on the dead man.

"It ain't enough," he'd said, "not to go up against *him*."

Now Ken Hill stared at Carl Hamm, challenging him with his eyes.

"So go ahead, Carl," Hill said, "go ahead and make a decision."

"All right," Hamm said, thrusting his jaw out. "All right, I will."

Hill sat there staring at Hamm while the man struggled to make some sort of a decision.

"Okay," Hamm said, "okay . . . okay, I've made a decision."

"And what is it?" Hill asked.

"I've decided that . . . that *you'll* decide what we're gonna do next," Hamm said.

"All right then," Hill said. "Shut up and listen. Adams is gonna go for the gold after this."

"Why do you say that?"

"Because that's what *I'd* do," Hill said. "After two attempts to kill him, he's got to figure the only way to keep it from happening again is to go and find the gold."

"So what do we do about it?"

"That's simple," Hill said. "We get there ahead of him."

"Just the two of us?"

"We'll start out just the two of us," Hill said. "Along the way we'll pick up some help."

"Like those last three?"

"Guns," Hill said, "all we need are some more guns. The next time we go after Adams, I'll be calling the shots myself. With enough guns, we'll take care of him. Trust me."

Hamm frowned. *Could* he trust Ken Hill? That was something he'd find out as time went by.

TWENTY

At eight A.M. Monday morning Clint was in front of the Carlyle Hotel, waiting for Ben Schutz to come out. He had brought Duke, his big, black gelding, who had been stabled near the White Palace Hotel.

Already tied up in front of the hotel was a saddle horse and one pack mule. Clint checked the horse and found him sound. He was going over the supplies on the mule when Schutz appeared.

"Good morning, partner."

"Morning," Clint said.

"That's a beautiful horse," Schutz said, openly admiring Duke.

"Thanks."

"I hope mine can keep up."

"Yours will do fine," Clint assured him.

"Did I miss anything?" the big man asked, stepping down into the street. He stood next to Clint and looked at the supply-laden mule.

"Not that I can see," Clint said. He took a few more moments to check the supplies on the mule, then turned to Schutz. "We're pretty well outfitted . . . for one mule, that is."

"I thought we'd travel better with one pack animal," Schutz said. "I thought that should be a consideration, er, considering we might be followed and all."

"It's a good thought."

Clint noticed that there was a Winchester on the saddle horse, but that Schutz was not wearing a handgun.

"There's something we haven't discussed," Schutz said. "We should get it out of the way before we get started."

"What is it?"

"The split," Schutz said.

"The split?" Clint said. "Oh, you mean the split."

"Right," Schutz said, "right. How are we gonna split up the gold—*if* we find gold, that is."

"Well . . . fifty-fifty sounds fair to me," Clint said. "How about you?"

Schutz looked surprised.

"It's pretty generous, considering *you* have the map and *you're* the one who's been attacked twice over it," he said. "I was thinking sixty-forty . . . maybe."

"No," Clint said, shaking his head. "You'll be taking as big a chance as I am, plus you know your way around that region. No, fifty-fifty is fair enough."

"Okay," Schutz said, "okay. Now that we've got that settled, let's mount up."

"How far do you figure we have to go?" Clint asked as they mounted their horses.

"Oh, a hundred and twenty-five, maybe a hundred and fifty miles," Schutz said. "With the pack mule, and with some of the traveling being over mountains, I figure we'll be there in about ten or twelve days, depending on whether or not we push it."

"What's the best route?" Clint asked as they started riding.

"Well, just follow the Sacramento River," Schutz said. "That should take us to Shasta City. From there we start up Mount Shasta."

"That's where the mine is?"

"It is," Schutz said. "The map is not marked with names of places and rivers, but I recognize the Sacramento River, and Shasta City, and some of the other landmarks."

"You see?" Clint said. "You're earning your fifty percent already."

"I just wish it was all going to be this easy," Schutz said.

They both knew there was *no* chance of that.

TWENTY-ONE

Two days out of Sacramento they were camped along the banks of the Sacramento River. It was dark, and Schutz was burning the bacon again.

"Can *never* get this right," he complained.

They'd agreed to share the cooking, even though neither was a great cook. As it turned out, Schutz couldn't even make bacon without burning it, but still insisted on sharing the cooking.

At least there wasn't much he could do to ruin the coffee. On the trail it usually came out hot, black, and strong, which was just the way Clint liked it.

Schutz looked up and saw Clint staring out into the dark the way they had come.

"What is it?"

"We're being followed."

"How long?"

"Most of the past two days."

Schutz stood up and walked over to stand by him. "You never said anything."

"I knew," Clint said. "That was enough."

"Is it them?"

Clint shook his head.

"I don't think so," Clint said. "Near as I can figure, it's only one rider."

76

"Maybe they sent someone on ahead to keep track of us," Schutz suggested.

"That's possible," Clint said. "But he's not doing much to hide himself—whoever it is."

"Really?" Schutz said. "And I didn't have a clue. I've been off the trail too long, I guess. Holed up in a hotel room too long."

Clint looked at his new partner and said, "I been meaning to ask you about that."

"About what?"

"About *why* you've been holed up in a hotel room for . . . for how long?"

Schutz shrugged and said, "A long time. Maybe when we've been partners a little longer I'll tell you about it. Okay?"

"Sure," Clint said, abiding by the man's wishes.

"What do we do about this?" Schutz asked. He used his chin to indicate whoever it was behind them.

"Well," Clint said, "we could just let him keep following us, or I could go out there and find out who it is."

"In the dark?"

Clint looked at Schutz and said, "That's the best time. He won't expect it."

"I haven't even seen a fire behind us, not last night or now," Schutz said.

"That's because whoever it is is making a cold camp," Clint said.

He turned, walked to his saddle, and picked up his rifle.

"I'll be right back," he said.

"Be careful, Clint," Schutz said. "Like I said, I've been off the trail a long time. I kind of like the company, you know?"

"Like I said," Clint repeated, "I'll be right back— and maybe with company."

"I'll put on more bacon."

"No," Clint said, "do me a favor . . . don't . . ."

Clint moved through the darkness as quietly as he could, but he didn't think he'd be detected. From what he had already observed of the person following them, whoever it was was not exactly at home out here. In fact, Clint was sort of surprised that he hadn't gotten lost before now. Approaching him now was simply to satisfy his own curiosity.

Soon enough he came upon the cold camp. One lone figure was sitting on the ground with a blanket around him. Nearby a horse had been improperly picketed, so that at any moment he might bolt and break loose, leaving the person on foot. Clint toyed with the idea of *making* the horse bolt, then decided against it—at least until he found out just *who* the person was.

He moved up behind the seated figure and then, in one swift movement, grasped the bottom of the blanket and pulled it up and over his head.

"Hey!" a muffled voice called out in surprise. The figure started to flail about, trying to get out from under the heavy blanket.

Clint stuck his hands beneath the blanket, looking for a gun and not finding one. His hands tried to tell him something as he groped the person's body, but his head refused to believe it.

There was a rifle on the nearby saddle, and he took a quick step and picked it up. By the time the person had extricated himself from the blanket, Clint was covering him with his own rifle.

"All right, friend," Clint said. "Start talking. What's your story? Why are you following us?"

"Because you were too stubborn to take me with you willingly," Patsy Kelly said, glaring up at him, "that's why . . . *friend*!"

TWENTY-TWO

Angrily, Clint led Patsy and her horse back to camp, where Schutz was busily burning bacon to a crisp.

"See?" she said to him as they entered camp. "It *smells* like you need me."

Clint didn't answer.

Schutz looked up from the smoke that was coming up from the frying pan, and stared at Patsy in surprise.

"A woman, huh?" he asked. "What will they think of next. A female killer."

"It's you who are a killer," Patsy said.

"What?"

"You're killing that bacon," she said. "Do you have any more?"

"We have plenty."

"You won't if you keep burning it," she said, elbowing him aside. "Here, let me do it."

Schutz backed away from the fire as Patsy took over. She started laying bacon into the frying pan strip by strip.

"Is she a friend of yours?" Schutz asked Clint.

"She *was*," Clint said.

Schutz gave the annoyed Clint an amused look and asked, "A *good* friend?"

"We'll talk about it later," Clint said. "Here, take care of her horse."

He gave Schutz the horse's reins, and then took the saddle from his shoulder and handed that over too. The big man handled it one-handed with more ease than Clint had with two hands.

"Don't kill her," Schutz said, "until *after* she cooks dinner."

As Schutz walked away with the horse and saddle, Clint confronted Patsy across the fire. He was distracted by the smell of *properly* cooking bacon.

"How could you do this?" he asked.

"It was easy," she said. "Well, it *wasn't* really easy. A couple of times I thought I lost you—and then *I* would have been lost."

"It would serve you right if you *did* get lost," Clint scolded her. "What were you thinking about?"

"I was thinking about getting out of Sacramento for a while," she said. "I was thinking about getting away from Babe's for a while. I was thinking about *us*."

"Patsy," Clint said, shaking his head, "this is dangerous."

"*Life* is dangerous, Clint," she said. "Look at you. You were minding your own business, having breakfast, and look what you got yourself into."

"Right," he said, "I got *myself* into it—and now I've gotten *you* into it."

"That's where you're wrong," she said. "Anything I've ever done I got *myself* into—including this. You can't take the blame for this."

"All right, I won't," he said. "Whatever happens to you from here on, it is *your* fault."

"I can live with that," she said.

"I sincerely hope so," he said. He sniffed at the

bacon and grudgingly asked, "When will dinner be ready?"

"Soon," she said. "Do you have any beans?"

"Yes."

"Biscuits?"

"Yes."

"And coffee."

"Of course."

She grinned to herself and said, "Of course."

Schutz came walking over and said to Clint, "Got it all straightened out?"

"No," Clint said. "She's coming with us."

"And doin' the cookin'?" Schutz asked.

"Yes," Clint said, "and doing the cooking."

"I can live with that," Schutz said, rubbing his hands together.

Clint looked at him and said, "Oh, shut up."

TWENTY-THREE

After he had calmed down a bit—aided by a good dinner and trail coffee that Patsy had somehow made taste better—Clint asked her some questions about the past two days.

"Did you notice anyone behind you?" he asked.

"I didn't see anyone," she said, and then admitted, "I *was* looking *ahead* of me very intently, though."

"All right, what about *ahead* of you?" he asked. "Anyone between you and us that I might have missed?"

She shook her head. "No, Clint," she said, "I didn't see anybody. Why?"

"Clint thinks that someone should be following us," Schutz said.

"Someone besides me, you mean," Patsy said.

"Right," Schutz said.

"Well," she said, looking at both of them wide-eyed and innocent, "maybe they're *ahead* of you?"

Clint looked at Schutz, who stared back at him and then shrugged.

"That's very good, Patsy," Clint said.

"Really?"

"I'm serious," Clint said. He looked at Schutz. "They're ahead of us. They're trying to get there first."

"Without the map?"

"Maybe they have another map."

"Then why try so desperately to get *this* copy?" Schutz asked.

"So that no one else will have one," Clint said. "Or maybe they've seen the map and know the way without it."

"So after trying for the map several times, they finally decide to just go on ahead and get there before anyone else," Schutz said.

"Right."

Schutz nodded and said, "It makes sense." He looked at Patsy and asked, "Does she know what this is all about?"

"Yes," Clint said, and then explained that he had hidden the map with Patsy and that he'd felt she'd deserved an explanation.

"I don't have a problem with that," Schutz said. "Can she shoot?"

"That subject never came up between us," Clint said. He looked at her and asked, "Can you?"

"With a rifle, yes," she said. "With a pistol, I'm helpless. That's why I didn't bring one."

"What is it about pistol shooting that's making it a lost art?" Clint asked.

"It's just easier to aim a rifle," Patsy said with a shrug.

"I agree," Schutz said.

"You don't aim a pistol," Clint said, "you just *point* it, as if it was your finger. If you do that, you can hit what you're pointing at."

"Maybe *you* can," Patsy said.

"*We* can't," Schutz said, and he and Patsy shared a look and a nod of assent.

"All right," Clint said, "at least you can both shoot a rifle."

"I've never shot *at* anybody before," Patsy said.

Clint looked at Schutz.

"Oh, I have . . ." he said.

"Good."

"But I've never actually *hit* anybody," Schutz added.

Clint poured himself some more coffee and didn't say anything. It was clear that if and when they ran into trouble it was going to fall to him to get them out of it. At least Patsy and Schutz would be able to make some *noise,* make it *sound* like they were better armed than they actually were.

TWENTY-FOUR

A couple of days ahead of Clint, Ben Schutz, and Patsy, Ken Hill and Carl Hamm camped.

"How far behind us do you think he is?" Hamm asked Hill.

"Who knows?" Hill said. "All we really know is that we left before him. He could be an hour behind us, or a week."

"I hope it's a week," Hamm said. "I hope we can get enough gold out of that mine and be gone before he gets there."

"Hamm," Hill said, "how long do you think it takes to get gold out of a mountain?"

"I don't know," Hamm said with an indifferent shrug of his shoulders.

"Do you know *anything* about gold mining?" Ken Hill asked.

"No."

"Well, I do," Hill said, "so stop making stupid remarks about it."

"Hey," Hamm said, "what'd I say?"

"We're not gonna get enough gold out of that mine until it's *dry*," Hill said, "*completely* dry, do you understand that?"

Carl Hamm understood the words. What he didn't understand was the feverish gleam in the eyes of Ken Hill. He'd never seen *that* before on *any* man.

"Hello the camp?" a voice called out.

Ken Hill and Carl Hamm both looked up and out into the darkness.

"You think it's him?" Hamm asked in a whisper.

"If it was him," Hill said, standing up, "would he announce himself?"

Hamm frowned and said, "I guess not . . ."

"Hello the camp. Can we come in?"

"How many of you are there?" Hill called out.

"Three," the man said, "and we'll pay for some grub and some coffee."

Hill rubbed his jaw thoughtfully. Three?

"Come ahead," he said. "We've got all the grub you can eat."

"We do?" Hamm said.

"Shut up, Carl!" Hill hissed as the three men slowly entered the camp. They were on foot, leading their horses. "Let me handle this."

As it turned out, the intention of the three men was to rob Hill and Hamm. At least, that was their *original* intention. After Ken Hill finished talking—and Carl Hamm had to admit the man *could* talk—the three men were convinced that there was one man further behind them who had much more that was worth robbing than these two did.

"All we've got is grub and coffee," Hill told them, "and we're willing to *give* that to you."

"And what does this *other* fella have?" Dave Gallagher asked.

Gallagher was the spokesman for the three, if not the leader. As far as Hill could see, when it came to brains there wasn't much separating the three.

Hill looked at Gallagher and the other two and said, "Money, and plenty of it."

"How do you know this?"

"We tried to ride with him," Hill said, "but he chased us off. Tried to kill us. Shouted at us that we didn't have a chance at stealing his money."

"Is that so?" Gallagher asked, exchanging glances with his two friends.

"We're not handy with guns," Hill said, "so we kept on running."

"Well," Gallagher said, "we're pretty handy with guns ourselves."

"That's what I figured," Hill said.

At least, it was what he *hoped*.

TWENTY-FIVE

The next four days were pretty uneventful for the trio of Adams, Schutz, and Patsy Kelly.

The only thing that happened was that Ben Schutz and Patsy Kelly became very friendly. Oh, there was nothing romantic about it. Patsy still had her eye on Clint, and was waiting for a chance to crawl into his blankets with him. It was just that she and Ben actually got to be genuine friends, and they'd talk for hours on end while they were riding—all of which suited Clint just fine. It left him free to watch their backtrail, and to also keep an eye out up ahead.

On the night of their sixth day out of Sacramento Schutz said, "We need some more supplies, Clint. We've got about a day's worth left."

Water was no problem, since they were following the Sacramento River, but everything else was running very short.

Clint didn't need to question why. If it had been just the two of them they would have had plenty, but the third mouth to feed had put a strain on their supplies. Also, Schutz had burned a lot of bacon.

"Is there anyplace up ahead where we can get some?" Clint asked.

Schutz shook his head. "Not if we keep following the river," he said. "The only way we'll come to a settlement or a trading post is to move away from the river."

"That'll add some time to our trip," Clint said.

"It can't be helped."

"Can we ration?"

"If we were going to do that," Schutz said, "we should have started days ago."

"Good point," Clint said.

He didn't like adding even one day to their travel time. It would give the others even more of a head start on them. There didn't seem to be anything for it, though. They were going to *have* to stop for supplies.

"All right," Clint said. "You take the lead, Ben."

"Right."

Clint walked over to the fire to tell Patsy what was going on. She listened intently, which was something Clint had learned about her over the past four days. She listened, and she learned, and had done absolutely nothing to slow them down. Still, he wished she hadn't come along.

First of all, she was bound to end up in danger, and since he had to watch out for *her*, he might take less care with *himself*.

Secondly, she was a distraction. She was *there*, and he knew what she was like in bed, and he *wanted* her. With Schutz along, though, it just wasn't feasible for them to start sharing the same blanket every night. It just wasn't something that they could expect him to put up with.

"I guess this is my fault," she said when he was finished.

"There's no *fault*, Patsy," he said. "If there was, it would be mine."

"Why yours?"

"When you joined up I should have known we'd go through these supplies faster than we'd anticipated. I should have started us rationing supplies days ago."

"No," she said, shaking her head, "it's still my fault. I'm sorry, but—"

"All right, never mind," Clint said. "Let's not go into that. We're traveling as partners now, so we'll do what we have to do, and that means stopping for supplies."

"All right," she said. She looked down at the frying pan and said, "Tell Ben that dinner is ready."

Clint nodded, and went to tell Ben just that.

Dave Gallagher had sent Beau Canari on ahead to scout out the area, while he and Bob Trappman rode along at a more leisurely pace.

"You think those jaspers were tellin' us the truth?" Trappman asked.

"What if they weren't?" Gallagher said. "All they *had* was food and coffee, and we got all that we needed from them, didn't we?"

"Yeah," Trappman said, "but it ain't the same when they *give* it to you. You know what I mean?"

Gallagher laughed. He knew exactly what Bob Trappman meant. He, Trappman, and Canari had been riding this area for the past eight months, taking what they needed from travelers they met along the way, and *enjoying* every minute of it.

"It don't make a difference, Bob," Gallagher said. "Those two were mad as wet hens over what that other fella did to them. Yeah, I think they was telling the truth. I don't know if that fella really has money or not, but I guess that's something we're gonna find out, ain't it?"

At that moment Beau Canari appeared, riding back towards them. Both Gallagher and Trappman

reined in their mounts and waited for him to reach
them.

"What'd you find?"

"There's two men," Canari said, "and they're
traveling with a woman."

"A woman, huh?" Trappman said, his eyes suddenly gleaming.

Canari grinned at Trappman and said, "A good-
lookin' woman, Bob."

"Hey," Trappman said, nudging Gallagher with
his elbow, "this might end up bein' worth it after
all."

"Yeah," Gallagher said. Trappman liked taking
somebody's *woman* more than he liked taking his
money. Gallagher liked women, but he couldn't
understand that.

He looked at Canari and said, "Did they see
you?"

"No."

"You sure?"

"Sure I'm sure, Dave."

"Don't lie to me, Beau."

"I ain't lyin', Dave," Canari said. "Christ, one lie
and you're all over me all the time now."

"Yeah, well, *that* little lie almost got us killed,
remember?" Trappman asked.

"I ain't lyin' *this* time," Canari said.

"Okay," Gallagher said. "Are they headin' this
way?"

"Nope," Canari said, "they look like they're
headin' for Caxton's."

Caxton's was Caxton's Trading Post, a broken-
down post that had done a booming business during the Gold Rush, but now just barely got by. Still,
it was the only place in these parts where a body
could get supplies.

"They need supplies," Gallagher said. "That

means *we* head for Caxton's and get there ahead of them."

Trappman laughed, looked at Canari, and asked, "A *good*-lookin' woman, huh?"

Canari laughed and said, "A *real* good-lookin' woman!"

TWENTY-SIX

"That's Caxton's," Ben Schutz said, pointing. "It's been called Caxton's Hole, Caxton's Fort, and Caxton's Trading Post."

"And now?" Patsy asked.

"Now," Schutz said, "it's just called Caxton's."

She stared down at the ramshackle building, which looked like it was sitting in a hole, and said, "It looks more like Caxton's Hole."

"Well," Schutz said, "let's hope that it *is* still Caxton's at least."

"What else would it be?" she asked.

"Empty," Clint said.

They rode down to Caxton's, which wasn't really in a hole. It was more like a basin. When it rained it would have flooded if it hadn't been for the fact that there were two naturally formed runoffs on two sides of the post.

"That's why Caxton never had any trouble keeping this place," Schutz said. "Nobody else wanted to take a chance on the flooding. See, he knew the water would run off, but nobody else did."

"How do *you* know about it?" Patsy asked.

Schutz looked at her and said, "Wade Caxton and I were once partners."

"What other surprises do you have in store?" Clint asked.

"If there are other surprises," Ben Schutz said, "they're not mine."

He didn't know how true his words were.

When they reached the building Schutz and Patsy dismounted, but Clint looked around, remaining astride Duke. The big black gelding was acting up, and there could only be one reason for that.

"What's wrong?" Schutz asked.

"I don't know," Clint said, patting the big gelding's neck, "but *something* is. Duke's agitated."

"Maybe he's got a stone bruise," Schutz said.

As the big man mounted the steps and started towards the door Clint called, "Ben, damn it, don't go in there yet!"

"Caxton, you old reprobate!" Schutz shouted, ignoring him. "Where are you?"

"Goddamnit!" Clint said, frustrated. "Patsy, stay with the horses."

"But Clint—"

"Do as I say!" he snapped, dropping down to the ground. "Stay here!"

"All right!"

Schutz had already gone through the front door, and Clint had no choice but to go in after him.

As he entered, his worst fears were realized. Ben Schutz was standing in the middle of the floor. Next to him stood a man who was holding a gun to the big man's head. He was also grinning at Clint, as if *daring* him to do something about it.

"Hi there," the man said to Clint. "Welcome to Caxton's. Leave your money on the counter, if you don't mind."

Clint looked around. There was another man off to the right. He was leaning against the wall, watching with an amused look.

From outside Clint heard Patsy shout, "Clint!"

As Clint turned, the man against the wall said, "Don't worry. Our friend will take care of her. He *likes* pretty girls."

The man with the gun laughed and said, "He likes them a *lot*."

"What do you fellas want?" Clint asked.

"My friend here already told you," the man against the wall said. "We want your money."

"What makes you think we've got any money?" Clint asked.

"A couple of friends of yours told us," the man with the gun said, but the other man cut him off before he could go further.

"Shut up, Beau!" he said. He looked at Clint and said, "You're here to buy supplies, aren't you?"

"So?"

"So what do you use to *buy* supplies, my friend?" the man asked. "Money."

"What's your name?" Clint asked.

The man against the wall looked surprised at the question. "Gallagher," he answered.

That was when Clint knew that these men fully intended to kill them. That meant that time was running out.

Schutz was unarmed. He had left his rifle outside. God only knows what was happening to Patsy. Clint had to move, and he had to move now.

"Didn't you ever hear of barter?" Clint asked.

"What?" Gallagher asked.

"Trade," Ben Schutz said. "We were gonna trade with Caxton."

"By the way," Clint said, "where *is* Caxton."

"He's in the back," Gallagher said.

"Alive?"

Gallagher just smirked.

"Anyway," Clint said, "since we were going to

trade for supplies, that means that we don't have any *money*. Whoever told you that lied to you, probably to save themselves from being robbed."

They heard some noise in the back, and then Clint heard Patsy cry out.

"Our friend is just gettin' cozy with your girlfriend," Gallagher said.

Obviously there was a back way, and the third man had brought Patsy into the back room to have his fun. At least now Clint knew where she was.

"I don't believe you," Gallagher said. "Empty your pockets on the counter."

"Don't you want to take my gun first?" Clint asked Gallagher.

Gallagher stood up straight and took out his own gun, pointing it at Clint.

"Why, are you dumb enough to draw on two already *drawed* guns?" Gallagher asked.

"I might be," Clint said, looking at Ben Schutz, "if I had some help!"

"What?" Gallagher asked.

"Aw, kill him," the man holding the gun on Schutz said, but suddenly Schutz moved faster than Clint thought the big man could. He grabbed the gunman's wrist and pulled it up so that his gun was pointing at the ceiling.

"Hey!" Gallagher shouted, taking his eyes off Clint for just a second—which was all Clint needed. He drew and fired in one motion. The bullet struck Gallagher squarely in the chest and slammed him back against the wall.

Clint didn't wait to see him fall. He rushed past Schutz and the other man to the back room. When he entered, the first thing he saw was a man's naked butt. The man—who had been trying to climb atop Patsy Kelly—had obviously heard the shot, and he was trying to pull his pants up.

The man looked behind him at Clint and said, "Shit!"

"Don't," Clint said, but the man released his pants and dove for his gun, which was in his holster on a nearby stack of grain bags.

Clint fired, and the man sprawled across the bags, bare-assed and dead.

"Jesus," Patsy said, getting to her feet. Her shirt was torn open and her breasts were naked and heaving. "It took you long enough!"

"I thought you'd be able to handle yourself," he said. "Look around back here. Caxton's supposed to be here somewhere—alive, I hope."

"I'll look around, all right," she said, "for a new shirt."

Before looking, though, she took one step and kicked the dead man right in the ass!

TWENTY-SEVEN

Clint turned and went back into the front room, where Ben Schutz was still holding the third man by the wrist. The man was actually *dangling* from Schutz's grasp, his feet inches off the floor.

"Jesus," he cried out in pain, "you're *crushin'* my wrist."

He had already dropped his gun to the floor.

"Let him down, Ben," Clint said, holstering his gun. "I want to ask him some questions."

Schutz opened his hand and let the man fall to the floor. He sat there and cradled his crushed wrist in his lap.

"Jesus, oh, sweet Jesus . . ." he said, rocking back and forth.

Clint knelt by him and said, "If you lie to me, I'll let my friend crush your other wrist." He poked the man and asked, "Do you understand me?"

The man nodded jerkily.

"Tell me who told you about us?"

"Two men."

"What two men?"

"I don't know what two men," he said. "Just two men we was gonna rob. They told us all they had was food and coffee, but that *you* had money. That

98

one of you did. That there was one fella alone who had money."

Clint looked at Schutz, then nudged the man again and said, "Keep talking."

The man went on to tell Clint everything that Hill and Hamm had told him and his partners, and how he and his partners had seen Clint, Ben, and Patsy together and had gone ahead to Caxton's.

"What were the names of those two men?"

"We never asked," the man said, "and they never told us. Jesus, my wrist hurts."

Clint stood up.

"At least you're alive to hurt," he said. "That's more than can be said for your partners."

At that moment Patsy came out of the storeroom with a man who looked to be in his sixties and had a weathered, wrinkled face. Patsy was wearing a new shirt that was too large for her, but it was buttoned and her breasts were covered.

"Caxton, you old coot!" Schutz said.

"Oh, no," Caxton said. "Don't tell me I got *you* to thank for saving my life."

"Well . . . actually it was my friend here," Schutz said.

"Well, thanks be for that," Caxton said. He looked at Clint and said, "Anything in the store is yours, mister."

"Thanks," Clint said. "The lady will tell you what we need while Ben and I clean up the mess we made."

Outside, Clint Adams lit into Ben Schutz.

"Don't *ever* do that again!"

"Do what?" Schutz asked. "How was I to know somebody was inside?"

"I was trying to *tell* you something was wrong," Clint said. "*You* weren't listening. You just *charged* right in without listening."

"All right!" Schutz said. "In the future I'll listen to you when you say your *horse* thinks there's something wrong. Jesus!"

"My *horse* has more sense than you do," Clint said. "He's saved my life more than once because he *thought* something was wrong."

Schutz remained silent for a moment, then said, "Clint, I'm sorry."

"All right, forget it now," Clint said. "Let's get those bodies out of there."

"What about the third man?"

"What about him?"

"Well . . . he was gonna *kill* me. What do we do with him?"

"Is there any law around here?" Clint asked.

"No."

"Do you want to take him to Shasta with us?"

"No."

"Do you want to turn around and take him back to Sacramento?"

"No."

"Then we let him go."

"But . . ."

"Or you can kill him," Clint said. "I'll leave the choice up to you."

Clint started to walk back inside, then turned suddenly and said, "Can I ask you something?"

"Sure," Schutz said. "You not only saved old Caxton's life, but mine as well—and probably Patsy's."

"And my own," Clint said. "Don't forget that."

"What'd you want to ask me?" Schutz asked.

"Did you *intentionally* crush that man's wrist?" Clint said.

"No," Schutz said, "I just didn't want him to shoot me."

Clint nodded, said, "That's what I thought," and then turned and went inside.

Talk about not knowing your own strength!

TWENTY-EIGHT

Patsy made all the arrangements for supplies with Caxton, and when Clint and Schutz had disposed of the dead bodies by dumping them *away* from the building, they returned and loaded the supplies onto the mule. They didn't take the time to actually *bury* the dead men, and felt no guilt about it. After all, those men were going to kill *them*, and it was doubtful that a decent burial had been part of their plan.

As for the third man, they allowed him to mount his horse—with a lot of difficulty, thanks to his broken wrist—and ride off in search of a doctor. The nearest one, according to Caxton, was a hundred miles away.

Once the supplies were loaded they went back inside to settle up with Caxton.

"No money," Caxton said, waving his hands at them. "You saved my life. How could I take money from *you*?" He was looking directly at Clint.

"How about me?" Schutz asked.

Caxton looked at him and said, "*You* I can take money from."

Schutz turned to Clint and Patsy and said, "I'll be right out."

Outside, Clint turned to Patsy and said, "Are you all right?"

102

"I'm fine . . . now," she said. "I was scared to death back there, though."

"That's understandable."

"It's not that he was gonna rape me," she said. "*That* I could have lived with. No, it's that I *knew* he was gonna kill me when he was done with me. I mean, he *told* me he was gonna kill me, and he was laughing about it."

Clint could see that reliving it was getting her agitated, and that she wasn't as "fine" as she'd claimed.

"Easy, Patsy . . ."

"I mean," she said, "until you've had someone *tell* you they're gonna kill you, you can't understand what it *feels* like."

She looked at him then and said, "Why am I telling you this? You've had people trying to kill you all your life, haven't you?"

"Well . . . most of it."

"How can you live like that?" she asked. She didn't wait for an answer. "Where do men like that one *come* from? Can you tell me that?"

"No," he said, "I can't."

She remained silent for a few moments, and he could see that she was trying to get herself under control—and she was doing it. He admired her for that.

She looked at him then and said, "You thought I was going to go crazy right then, didn't you?"

"The thought crossed my mind, yes," he said.

"Well, I'm not," she said. "I probably won't sleep too well for a while, but I'm not going to let what happened drive me crazy."

"I admire you for that, Patsy."

"You do?" she asked, looking surprised.

"Yes, I do."

"I'm not going to go back, you know."

"There's no reason for you to go back," he said. "You've been more than pulling your weight, and after what you've just been through I wouldn't ask you to go back."

"You mean . . . I earned the right to keep going?" she asked.

"Earned it, and more," he said, and he took her in his arms then and held her tightly. She leaned into him and, just for a moment, allowed herself the luxury of crying.

"Am I interrupting anything?" Schutz asked, coming out of the trading post.

"No," Patsy said, moving away from Clint and brushing at her eyes, "we're done."

"We're done here too," Schutz said.

"Time to start moving," Clint said. "Let's mount up."

Riding away from Caxton's, they discussed what had just happened.

Obviously, the two men from Sacramento *were* ahead of them, and had somehow convinced *these* three men that Clint was worth robbing. They also probably knew that these men would not only rob him, but kill him as well.

"They're ahead of you," Schutz said, "they're going to get there first, and they're *still* worried about killing you."

"And now you," Clint said.

"Yeah, now me," Schutz said. "And also Patsy. Maybe she should go back to Sacramento while she can."

Patsy looked at Clint, who looked at Schutz and said, "We already talked about that."

"And?"

"And she's staying."

"Fine with me," Schutz said. "I don't want to go back to burning bacon anyway."

They rode on in silence for a while, and then Patsy spoke up.

"There's something I don't understand," she said.

"What's that?" Clint asked.

"Well, even if most of Shasta is played out and there's no gold, and these fellas *do* find a mine shaft that *does* have gold . . . I mean, if they get there first and stake a claim, there's not much we can do about it, is there?"

"Not legally," Schutz said.

"What's that mean?" she asked, looking at both men. "Are we gonna try to take it away from them?"

"Well," Schutz said, "we do have the map."

"That shouldn't matter," she said. "I mean, if they get there first the claim is theirs, right?"

"Getting there first," Clint said, "is not going to stop *them* from trying to kill *us*."

"Does that justify us killing *them*?" she asked. "I mean, just to get the mine?"

"No," Clint said, "that only justifies us killing them in self-defense . . . if it comes to that."

"So then, we're not really gonna do anything *illegal*, right?"

"I don't plan to," Clint said. "How about you, Ben?"

Schutz shrugged, and didn't look at either one of them when he answered. He kept his eyes straight ahead. "Sure wasn't part of *my* original plan."

They went a few miles before Clint realized that Schutz had never really answered the question.

Ken Hill reined in his horse and stared off into the sky. Carl Hamm didn't realize it at first, and continued riding on. When he realized that Hill wasn't next to him any longer, he stopped his horse and turned in his saddle. He saw Hill staring with a faraway look in his eyes.

"What's the matter?" Carl Hamm asked. "What's wrong, Ken?"

"It didn't work," Hill said.

"What didn't work?"

Hill didn't look at Hamm when he answered. "Those three that we sent after Clint Adams," he said. "They didn't get the job done."

Ramm stared at Hill. "Uh, how can you know that, Ken?" he asked. "We haven't heard anything."

"I feel it," Hill said, and then he turned and looked at Hamm. "I can *feel* him behind us, Carl. Can't you feel it too?"

Hamm gave Hill a strange look and said, "Uh, no, Ken, I can't feel it."

Hill turned his head and looked off into the distance again.

"That's okay, Carl," he said. "I can feel it for both of us."

With that he started his horse again and moved past Carl Hamm, who stared after him, helplessly shaking his head.

Jesus, he thought, Hill was getting *scarier* by the minute.

TWENTY-NINE

"There it is," Ben Schutz said.

"There what is?" Patsy asked.

"Shasta City," Schutz said.

"It doesn't look like much of a city to me," she pointed out—and she was *more* than right.

"It's burnt out," Schutz said.

"I don't see any evidence of a fire," Patsy said seriously.

"That's not what he means," Clint said. "He means that, little by little, after the Gold Rush was over, people just started to leave. As a result it's just a shell of what it once was."

"I'll say," Patsy said. "Are we going there?"

Clint looked at Schutz and said, "We have to, don't we? For supplies?"

"Our supplies are okay," Patsy said.

"Not those kind of supplies," Clint said. He looked at Schutz again and asked, "What about the supplies we'd need for the gold?"

"I've got a pickax on the mule, Clint," Schutz said. "That's really all I need to determine whether or not there's gold. There's no point in lugging supplies up the mountain if it turns out there *is* no gold."

"What if there *is* gold?" Patsy asked.

"Then I come down and get everything we need," Schutz said.

"We can also go up and see if there's anybody waiting for us there," Clint said.

Clint and Schutz exchanged a glance again and just about read each other's minds.

"What if Patsy stays here?" Schutz asked, giving voice to what they were both thinking.

"Oh, no," Patsy said.

"Patsy," Clint said, "if the two men *are* waiting for us up there, there's going to be trouble."

"Shooting," Schutz said.

"And if they have more help—"

"Forget it," Patsy said. "I'm not staying down here alone. What if you go up there and leave me down here, and *they're* down here and not up *there*?"

Schutz looked at Clint and said, "What?"

"She's coming with us."

"Oh," Schutz said, wheeling his horse around. "Why didn't she just say so?"

Further up the mountain Carl Hamm was cursing himself. He had followed Ken Hill all this way, from Sacramento to the Shasta Mountains, to find a hidden gold mine, and *now* Hill couldn't *find* it.

Hamm sat his horse and watched Ken Hill walking around on foot, in circles. Hill hadn't admitted it yet, but he was lost. Carl Hamm could see that, but what could he do? Even lost, Hill knew more about these mountains than *he* did. He *had* to stay with him.

"What about it, Ken?" Hamm asked.

"I know there's a landmark around here someplace," Hill said. "I just can't *see* it."

"We need the map," Hamm said. "I *knew* we would need the map."

"If we need the map," Ken Hill said, "we can get it with no problem."

"How?"

Hill turned and looked at Hamm. He walked over and stood directly in front of Hamm's horse.

"All we have to do is wait for Adams to get here," Hill said. "We'll bushwack him and take the map away from him."

Hill was still insisting that Adams had managed to escape the three men they had sent after him. He still insisted that he *felt* Clint Adams's presence behind them.

"Come on," Hill said. "At least I know a place where we can hide the horses and wait."

For want of something better to do, Carl Hamm once again followed Ken Hill.

THIRTY

Clint, Schutz, and Patsy camped on a shelf that night. They had collected material for a few camp fires before starting up the mountain, in case there wasn't enough along the way. Before long Patsy had dinner sizzling in the pan, and the smell of coffee filled the air.

"Here you go," she said, and handed Clint and Schutz a cup of coffee each.

"Thanks," Clint said, and Schutz nodded his thanks as well.

As she went back to the fire Clint and Schutz looked up the mountain.

"There are a million places that could be used for an ambush," Schutz said.

"It's a chance we'll have to take," Clint said. "Unless . . ."

"Unless what?"

"Come morning," Clint said, "I'll go up ahead on foot. You and Patsy follow, also on foot, leading the horses. If somebody *is* waiting for us along the way, I should be able to flush them out."

"I don't like it."

"Do you have a better idea?"

Schutz hesitated and then admitted, "No."

"Then we'll do it my way," Clint said.

They stood there looking up the mountain together.

"Will the animals be able to make it all the way up the mountain?" Clint asked.

"We'd make better time if we left them," Schutz said, "but I can find a route for them. That'll put us further behind you, though."

"Don't worry about it," Clint said. "This is what I do."

"What is what you do?" Patsy asked, coming up behind them.

Clint turned and said, "I eat everything you cook. Is it ready?"

"That's what I came over to tell you," she said, but she was frowning at him. She knew they were discussing something they didn't want her to hear about. "It's all ready."

"Come on," Schutz said, taking her gently by the arm. "I'm starved."

Clint remained there a moment, continuing to look up the mountain. In all likelihood the two men who had been trying to have him killed since they killed the little man, Mike Smith, were up there waiting for him. To date they had never actually made an attempt on him themselves. The question was, where were they waiting? Halfway up? Further along? Or had they found the actual mine and were they waiting there?

Clint took out the map and looked at it. It was the first time he had done so since they left Sacramento. Now that they were into the Shasta Mountains, the thing actually seemed a little simpler to read. He was still going to need Ben Schutz, though, to find the way to the mine.

He stared at the map, then refolded it thoughtfully and tucked it away. At no time in his past—

not even when the whole country was caught in the gold fever—had *he* ever been caught up in it. He'd never had those visions of finding gold and being rich and living easy for the rest of his life. When he *had* a vision of getting rich, it was always at a poker table. There were no maps involved, and there was certainly less hard work and also less risk.

He looked around and wondered where he could find a decent poker game.

Patsy looked over to where Clint Adams was standing. He had not joined them to eat yet. He just stood looking up at the mountain, in the direction they had to go come morning.

"I wonder what he's thinking so hard about," she said to Schutz.

The big man shrugged and said, around a mouthful of bacon and beans, "Maybe he's planning what he's gonna do with his share of the gold."

Patsy stared at Schutz for a few moments, considering, then shook her head and looked back at Clint, who was now walking towards them. She had seen gold fever before, and Clint Adams did not show *any* of the symptoms in even the minutest degree.

But Ben Schutz, whenever *he* talked about the gold, acquired a gleam in his eye and seemed to grow excited. It was certainly not gold *fever*, but at least he revealed *some* enthusiasm about it.

But not Clint.

So, was he standing there thinking about what he would do with his share of the gold?

"I don't think so," she said.

THIRTY-ONE

Clint and Ben set watches that night, insisting that Patsy did not have to stand watch. She tried to argue the point, saying that she had pulled her weight up to now, and why should it change? Clint finally decided to tell her the truth.

"You don't have any experience, Patsy," he said, "and our lives might depend on you hearing or seeing something . . . and you'll miss it."

She opened her mouth to argue again, then closed it and thought for a moment.

"I guess you're right," she finally said. "I can see your point. By insisting, I could end up endangering your lives."

"*All* our lives," Clint said. "I'm concerned for all of us."

"I know you are."

"Then we're agreed?" Clint asked. "Ben and I will split the watches?"

"Sure," she said, "but wake me early and I'll make us breakfast before we start up the mountain again."

Clint took the last watch, so it was he who woke Patsy the next morning. He was leaning over her, trying to wake her with words rather than shaking her. Obviously, she had already been awake and was lying waiting for him. When he leaned over she put her arms around his neck, drew him down to her, and kissed him hard. Her mouth was sweet and warm, and he leaned into the kiss for a moment before drawing back from her.

"What a sneak," he said.

"It was the only way I could think of to at least get a kiss out of you," she whispered.

He pinched her and said, "Well, now that you've got it you can get up and make breakfast."

She rubbed her butt where he pinched her and said, "I think you bruised me. Want to look?"

"Yes," he said sincerely, "but not now. Get up and make breakfast, woman!"

"Yes, sir!" she said mockingly.

Clint checked on the condition of the horses while she got breakfast started. When he smelled the coffee he walked over to the fire, and she had a cup poured for him. He accepted it and sipped it gratefully.

"You can wake Ben now," she said. "Breakfast is almost ready."

Clint nodded, accepted another cup of coffee from her, and carried it over to Ben's bedroll.

"Ben, wake up," he said. When Ben didn't move, he had to call out again and nudge the big man with his foot before he opened his eyes. Clint held the cup aloft where Ben could see it—like a carrot before a donkey—and Ben sat up and reached for it.

"Thanks."

It wasn't really cold, but they *were* in the mountains and there was a slight chill in the air. The coffee was very welcome.

"Breakfast is ready," Clint said. "I didn't have the heart to tell Patsy *not* to make it, but let's eat quickly because I want to get started."

"I'm comin', I'm comin'," Ben mumbled. "Now I know why I got off the trail and holed up in a hotel."

"Why?"

"No early mornings."

Actually, Clint realized that they all didn't have to eat quickly. *He* did because he was going to be heading out before them. Since he wouldn't have a horse to worry about, he would also be following a slightly different route than Ben and Patsy.

Clint accepted a plate from Patsy and worked his way through it quickly. While he was eating it occurred to him—much *too* late—that he should have started up the mountain even earlier, possibly before the other men ahead of them had even awakened. He was confident enough in himself that he thought he could have surprised them even if they had set up watches. That opportunity, however, was gone and there was no point in belaboring it. In fact, there was no point in *thinking* about it anymore.

It was time to do it.

It occurred to Carl Hamm, who was standing the last watch of the night, that he *could* have—and *should* have—taken his horse and gotten out of there, gotten *away* from Ken Hill before the man either drove him crazy or got him killed.

Of course, he had to consider that if he stayed, Ken Hill *might* make him a rich man. Carl Hamm had been struggling all of his life, even *before* his father died and it fell to him to support his mother and five brothers and sisters. He'd put up with *that* for five years, until he was seventeen years old, and then he'd just *left*. That was fifteen years ago, and his life had *not* improved the way he would have liked.

He had put up with a *lot* during his life, and if all he had to do was suffer Ken Hill for a few more days in order to get rich, he could do that.

Of course, there was also the fact that Carl Hamm—no gunman, certainly—was going to have to go up against Clint Adams, a notorious gunman. He only hoped that Ken Hill knew what he was doing, and that between them they could handle Clint Adams.

THIRTY-TWO

Clint found the early going fairly easy, and knew that behind him Schutz and Patsy Kelly would have no problem negotiating the way with the horses. He moved slowly, for there were many outcroppings of rocks and twists and turns that a man could hide behind. By noon, however, no one had materialized. He was starting to think—and hope—that perhaps the anticipated ambush would not take place. Perhaps the two nameless men who had been trying so desperately to steal the map had given up and returned to Sacramento.

Sure.

"How long do we sit here?" Hamm asked.

"Until Clint Adams shows up," Ken Hill said.

"What if he doesn't show up?"

"He will."

Hamm didn't like this. What if Adams had taken a different route. He might be ahead of them now, or he might even have found the mine already. Or someone *else* might have stumbled onto it. The longer they waited, the more of a chance there was that someone else would get there first. He decided to make a suggestion to Ken Hill that he *knew* the man would not agree to.

"Hill," he said, "what if one of us went up ahead and found the mine while the other one waited here for Clint Adams?"

Hill did not react at first, and then when he did he did it slowly, turning his head and eventually focusing his eyes on Hamm. "What?"

"I said—"

"I *know* what you said," Hill said.

He just stared at Hamm long enough for the other man to start to fidget.

"What?" Hamm said finally.

"Hamm," Hill said, "do you intend to steal from me?"

"No," Hamm said, as if the thought had *never* crossed his mind. Actually, it had, and now he was starting to wonder if Hill *knew* that it had.

"Do you *think* you could possibly steal from me?" Hill asked. His voice was as cold as steel.

Hamm opened his mouth to answer, wet his lips, and tried again. "N-no."

Hill leaned forward and said, "Don't *ever* think that you can steal from me, Hamm. It would never happen. You'd be dead before you knew what hit you."

"Ken," Hamm said, "I wasn't going to steal from you. I was just worried that someone would get there ahead of us and get the gold."

"Hamm," Hill said, "just do what I tell you and let me do the worrying. Understand?"

"Sure, Hill, sure," Hamm said. "I understand you."

"Good."

Hill turned his eyes away from Hamm, who felt as if he had been released physically. His shoulders slumped, and he let out a breath and felt his body relax.

• • •

Ken Hill was *anything* but relaxed.

He had been tense ever since Clint Adams had entered the situation. Smith had been easy to take care of. If it hadn't been for Adams they'd have the map by now. One thing Clint Adams had done, however, was get rid of one of his partners for him. When it came time to kill Carl Hamm, though, Hill was going to have to do it himself—and he might even find himself enjoying it.

The idea of being so close to the gold and not being able to find it was doing things to Ken Hill's mind. He had never been up here before, but it had been described to him in detail by an old-timer who had thought that Hill was going to help him get to the gold. Hill had helped him, all right. He'd milked the old man for all the information he could, and then killed him. Before he killed him, however, the old man had told him about the *other* man who had agreed to help him, a man named Mike Smith. Instead, Smith had stolen the map. So after killing the old man, Ken Hill had gone looking for Smith and the map.

That left them where they were today. He admitted to himself that he *couldn't* find the mine, so they *had* to wait for Adams to come along with the map.

Hill lifted his eyes for a moment and looked at the sky. He swept his eyes around, past Hamm—who flinched—and then suddenly stopped. Why hadn't he thought of that before?

"What is it?" Hamm asked, noticing the look on Hill's face.

Hill didn't answer right away, and he had a far-away look in his eyes.

"Hill?"

Suddenly, Hill's eyes seem to focus and he looked

directly at Hamm. "You know something, Carl?"

"What?"

"Your idea wasn't so bad after all."

THIRTY-THREE

Clint rested.

The going had become much steeper, but he had chosen a different route which he knew would leave Schutz, Patsy, and the animals behind. There was no way they would be able to follow the narrow, rocky route *he* was now following. The mule might be surefooted enough to make it, but certainly not the horses—and *most* certainly not Duke. The big gelding was just too big and heavy to even try it. At least, Clint *hoped* that Schutz wouldn't decide to try it.

Since he had taken to the new, much rockier route, Clint had stopped to rest several times. His legs were just not used to carrying him up a steep mountain incline for several hours, and whenever they rebelled he'd have to stop to give them a rest. Also, the higher he got the thinner the air got, which was taxing on his lungs.

During one of his rest stops he found himself looking out over the vista and at the sky, and he thought that the mountains would be a perfect place for a man to spend some time alone. Every time he'd ever tried to find someplace like that, he'd managed to get himself drawn into someone's business. Up here he'd be alone, with no such distractions around. After this was all over maybe he'd look into finding a mountain retreat somewhere—if not in these mountains, then somewhere else.

He stood up, stretched his muscles, and started his upward climb again. On occasion he'd come face to face with an obstacle that was impassable, unless he was a mountain goat, and he'd have to retrace his steps and find another way. Of course it would have been easier to go back to a main trail, but he was convinced that—if an ambush was in the works—the main trails were being watched. Maybe by taking these nearly impassable routes it would be *he* who would ambush *them*.

Carl Hamm cursed himself. It *had* been his idea for one of them to go on in search of the mine while the other stayed behind to ambush Clint Adams, but *he* had wanted to be the one who continued on. Now here he was, sweaty hands holding his rifle, waiting for Adams to appear, while Ken Hill had gone looking for the gold.

"I thought you couldn't find it," Hamm had said when Hill told him to stay.

"I want to give it another try," Hill had said. "Just *stay* here and wait for him. When he comes, kill him and then follow me."

"How am I gonna follow you?"

"I'll leave a trail for you to follow."

"How? What kind of trail?"

"I'll scratch an X in the rocks as I go along," Hill had said. He'd picked up a stone and bent down to scratch a barely legible X in the ground. "See?"

Hamm had stared, barely able to see it, but he'd nodded his head.

"What's the matter, Carl?" Hill had asked then. "Do you think I'm gonna steal from you?"

"No, Hill," Hamm had replied carefully, "no, of course I don't."

Hill had put his hand on Hamm's shoulder, and looked up and said, "I'll see you up there, Carl. By the time you get there we'll be rich."

Hamm thought about that now, while he continued to wait for Clint Adams. He thought about being rich, and what he would do with all that money.

Hell, it was better than worrying . . .

Ken Hill continued up the mountain, keeping his eyes ahead on the landmark he had finally managed to locate. He didn't know how he'd managed to miss it before, but it was there now, and he was keeping it in sight almost constantly, as if it might move away and hide from him when he wasn't looking.

The entire way he'd be keeping his ears open for shots. If Hamm killed Clint Adams, that would be fine. Hill would then kill Hamm when the other man joined him. If, on the other hand, Clint Adams managed to kill Hamm—and wasn't that more likely?—well, that wouldn't be so bad either. Hill would just have to kill Clint Adams himself.

He could do that, especially when you considered what was at stake.

"It's so quiet," Patsy Kelly said.

Ben Schutz didn't say anything.

"Isn't it?" she asked.

"What do you expect to hear, Patsy?"

"I don't know," she said. "I'm just worried about Clint."

"Clint will be fine," Schutz said. "Worry about these animals. If one of them slips and gets hurt, we're going to be in trouble."

"All right," she said.

Patsy was leading her horse and Schutz's horse, while Schutz led the mule and Clint's horse. The mule was the most important animal of the four, as far as their survival was concerned, but Ben knew how much the big gelding meant to Clint, so he'd chosen to handle those two animals while Patsy led the other two. To Schutz, a horse was just that, a horse, and Patsy certainly had no sentimental attachment to the animal she was riding.

"I just wish we'd hear something," Patsy said under her breath.

Schutz refrained from telling her that if and when they did hear something, it would probably be shots, and if they heard shots it would mean that Clint was in trouble.

No, Ben Schutz was hoping that they would hear nothing at all.

THIRTY-FOUR

Clint couldn't believe his eyes, or his luck.

As he climbed onto the ledge he saw the other man. He was facing away from Clint, watching the path intently—the path Clint would have been coming up if he hadn't chosen to get *off* the main path to find another way. Apparently, Clint's laborious routine, turning around when cut off and finding another route, had taken him *around* so that when he did make it to the ledge—or shelf— he came up *behind* the man who was waiting to bushwhack him.

The man's gun was still in his holster. There was a rifle leaning against a rock wall next to him. All Clint had to do was climb all the way up on the shelf, and then sneak up behind him. He would have been able to do that if his foot hadn't slipped on some loose rock. He lost his footing and slammed his knee painfully against the edge of the shelf. The pain shot through his knee and he lost his grip with his left hand. *That* caused him to cut the palm of his hand on a sharp outcropping of rock, and he cried out.

The man heard him and turned around quickly.

"What the hell—" the man said.

Clint braced his left elbow on the ledge and used it and his right hand to pull himself up. By then the man had his gun out, and all Clint could do was *roll* and try to avoid being shot.

Hamm, seeing the man climbing up onto the shelf, didn't recognize him at first. All he knew was that he had to shoot him. Even if it *wasn't* Clint Adams, they didn't need somebody else around who might want a piece of their mine.

He clawed for his gun, drawing it from his holster as quickly as he could. The man was rolling and Hamm fired, but damn it, he couldn't *hit* him.

"Stay still, damn it!" he shouted, pulling the trigger again and again until the hammer fell on empty chambers.

"Shit," he said.

Clint rolled and rolled, bruising his shoulders and elbows and knees—the damned *painful* knee! He heard the shots, and the lead striking the ground around him, and then he heard the click-click-click of a hammer falling on empty chambers. He stopped rolling and came to a stop, but he tried to plant his weight on the injured knee. The pain shot through his leg and he cried out again.

The other man dropped his handgun and reached for his rifle.

"Don't!" Clint wanted to shout. He opened his mouth, but he didn't know what came out. Maybe it was the word, maybe it was just a cry of pain. Whatever it was, the other man wasn't listening.

Clint drew his gun and fired. The bullet hit the man in the shoulder, causing him to drop the rifle and spin around. Clint watched helplessly as the man took a staggering step and his foot went completely *off* the shelf.

And then he wasn't there anymore.

Patsy heard the shot and jerked her head up.

"Ben," she said.

Before Schutz could speak, the other shots sounded, one right after the other.

They both listened until the shots stopped, and then looked at each other.

"What does it mean?" she asked.

Again, even before he could think of an answer, there was one more shot, and then nothing.

"Ben?" she said.

He looked at her and said, "He's fine."

Ken Hill heard the barrage of shots echoing up towards him and stopped to listen. Could it be possible that Hamm had successfully bushwhacked Clint Adams?

That was when he heard the next shot, just one, and he knew that Clint Adams was alive.

He looked up at his landmark and kept moving.

THIRTY-FIVE

"What do you mean, you think he's fine?" Patsy asked. "How can you say that after all that shooting?"

They had continued to walk, while discussing what they *thought* had happened.

"After all those shots, you heard that last one, right? After a pause?"

"So?"

"That was him," Schutz said. "He let the other man empty his gun and then he fired."

"Even if that's true," she said almost petulantly, "he could still be hurt."

"I know," he said, "that's why we're not stopping . . ."

Clint sat down on the shelf floor with his legs out in front of him. His left knee was throbbing, and his left palm was stinging. He still held his gun in his right hand. He looked at his gun, and then holstered it.

He pulled a handkerchief from his pocket and wrapped it tightly around his palm, then turned his attention to his injured knee.

Using both hands he lifted his leg, flexing the knee, and gritted his teeth at the pain. Christ, could you break a kneecap? Why not? It was a bone, wasn't it? No, it couldn't be broken, or he wouldn't be able to bend it.

The pants leg wasn't ripped, so there was no open wound. As he flexed the knee with his teeth clenched he realized that, at most, he had probably badly bruised the knee, but there was nothing broken.

Gingerly he made a move to get to his feet, but when he put his hands down for balance the pain in his left hand made him hiss.

As far as he could see, the man who had been shooting at him had fallen off the shelf. What he didn't know was how *far* he had fallen. It was possible that he had simply fallen to another ledge. If the man was still alive, it would be helpful. If he had fallen further—like completely *off* the mountain—then he was surely dead.

Moving slowly and carefully, Clint got to his feet and tested the knee. There was pain, but at least the leg held him. He took a few tentative steps, and hobbled over to the area from which the man had fallen. The man's gun was still on the ground where he had dropped it, but his rifle had fallen over with him.

Clint looked over the side. The man had not quite fallen *off* the mountain, but he had fallen far enough so that he looked very small and very dead.

"Shit," Clint said, and he sat down on the ground to wait for his friends.

It was hours before Schutz and Patsy caught up to Clint, but he just sat there waiting, trying to keep his hand from bleeding, and trying to exercise his knee gingerly so it wouldn't stiffen up completely.

When they came into view he was sitting on the ground, his legs out in front of him, cradling his blood-soaked hand in front of him.

"What took you so long?" he asked.

"Clint," Patsy said, and rushed to him. The relief in her voice was like a flood that washed out of her and over him.

Schutz, who didn't want Clint to know that he had been worried, said, "See? I told you he was all right."

Clint looked up at the big man, who added, "Fool woman thought you were hurt."

THIRTY-SIX

Patsy had glared at Schutz and said, "He *is* hurt," and had then washed the wound and bound it with clean cloth she had in her saddlebag.

Now they were camped on the shelf with a small fire going.

They had talked about the possibility of climbing down to where the man was, on the off chance he was still alive, but then decided against it. For one thing, Clint *couldn't* climb down because of his hand and knee. For another, Schutz was just too damned big to want to risk it.

"The only mountain climbing I do," he said, "is on a nice wide path. Besides, if he ain't dead he deserves to be. Forget about him."

"It's not that," Clint said. "Maybe we could get him to tell us where his partner went."

"We won't need him," Schutz said. "We have the map to show us the way."

It was too dark just then to take the map out and start looking for landmarks drawn on it, so they decided they would do that in the morning.

All three of them sat around the fire and discussed their trip so far, and what was going to happen next.

"The other man's obviously ahead of us," Ben

Schutz said. "He left this one behind to take care of you."

"Or to be taken care of *by* me," Clint said.

"You mean . . . he left that man here to be killed?" Patsy asked. "But why? Aren't they partners?"

"That's what this man thought," Clint said. "Obviously, the other man never intended to share the gold with *any* of his partners. That's why he sent them after me, and never came after me himself."

"He's afraid?" Patsy asked.

"Maybe," Clint said, "and maybe he's just . . . very smart."

"Smart?" she said.

"Sure," Schutz said. "He's using everyone. He wants his partners to try to kill Clint, or to be killed *by* Clint."

"And what happens when his partners are all gone?" Patsy asked.

Schutz looked at Clint and said, "When we find him he's gonna have to face Clint himself."

"But . . . if he *could* kill Clint, why hasn't he faced him by now?"

"Not until he has to," Schutz said. "He'll put it off as long as he can, but when the time comes he'll do it, all right. He's a smart one."

"Maybe," Clint said, looking up at the dark mountain, "but he's all alone now, isn't he?"

"Maybe that's what he wants," Patsy said. "He wants to be all alone in his gold mine."

"It's not his," Schutz said.

"It's not anybody's yet," Clint said. "Maybe it doesn't even exist."

"If it doesn't," Schutz said, "a lot of people have died for nothing."

"Nothing new," Clint said, shaking his head, "nothing new . . ."

• • •

They set up watches, just to be on the safe side. Schutz took the first watch, and when he woke Clint for his, Clint found that his knee had stiffened up badly.

"You're gimpy," Schutz said. "Maybe you shouldn't go any further."

"What do you suggest I do? Stay here?"

"It's a thought."

Clint grunted, rolled out of his blanket, and got to his feet. His knee buckled, and if not for Schutz he would have fallen.

"See what I mean?" Schutz said.

Clint pulled away from the man and stood on his own two feet.

"By morning I'll be mobile," Clint said. "I'll keep taking the last watch the rest of the way. That way by each morning I will have worked the stiffness out."

"Suit yourself," Schutz said. "I'm tired, I'm gonna get some rest. We stayin' together tomorrow?"

"Yes," Clint said. "I don't think this man is going to stop now for an ambush or for any reason."

"No," Schutz said, rolling himself up in his blanket, "neither do I. See you later."

"Right."

Clint went over and sat by the small fire. Once it started to die out he'd let it, so as not to waste whatever makings they had left. He'd spent plenty of nights in cold camps, and this would certainly not be the worst.

He kept his rifle nearby, and massaged his knee from time to time. When he became aware that someone was behind him he grabbed the rifle and turned, even though he *expected* it to be either Schutz or Patsy. As it turned out, it was Patsy Kelly.

"What are you doing up?" he asked.

"Couldn't sleep," she said. "Can I sit with you a while?"

"Sure," he said, and she sat next to him on the hard ground.

"How's your knee?" she asked.

"Fine."

"Liar," she said, and he took his hands away from his knee. "Let me see your hand."

He held it out. Blood had seeped through her bandage, and she decided to change it then and there.

"You can do it later," he said.

"I'm up now," she said. "I'll do it now."

Finally he agreed, and held out his hand while she removed the soiled bandage, cleaned the wound, and applied a clean cloth.

"There," she said, giving him back his hand.

"You'd better get some sleep," he said, flexing the hand.

"I'd rather stay here," she said, and leaned against him.

"That'd be . . . uncomfortable."

She giggled and said, "Am I making you uncomfortable, Mr. Adams?"

"Yes, damn it," he said, and kissed her. Their tongues touched, then entwined, and then he pulled his mouth away reluctantly.

"Go to bed," he said. "We have to save this for another time."

"Oh, all right," she said. She leaned against him heavily before getting up. Then she said, "Coward," and went back to her blanket.

THIRTY-SEVEN

In the morning Clint woke both Patsy and Schutz, and they decided not to waste time making coffee and breakfast. Instead they all ate beef jerky and water and hurriedly broke camp.

Once they were ready to go Clint produced the map, which he and Schutz examined.

"This is where we started, down near the bottom," Schutz said, pointing.

"I see it."

"We moved up along here . . ." he said, still moving his finger.

"So then, this is about where we are now," Clint said, pressing *his* finger to the map.

"Uh, yeah, right," Schutz said.

"What is *this*?" Clint asked.

"Peaks," Schutz said. "They're drawn to look like . . . like two fingers pointing at the sky. But all the peaks around here point at the sky."

"They do," Clint said, looking around, "but not like those."

"I don't—"

"There," Clint said, with just a hint of excitement. "Right there."

He pointed, and Schutz looked. Sure enough they saw two mountain peaks that were so slender and so close together they actually resembled fingers pointing at the sky.

"Fingers," Schutz said under his breath.

"Pointing the way," Clint said, folding the map. "That's the way we're headed."

"And the way our other friend is headed too," Schutz reminded him.

"Right."

"Are we going?" Patsy asked.

Clint tucked the map away in his pocket and said, "We're going."

They pushed on, with Clint refusing to ride Duke while Schutz led the big gelding. Clint walked with a limp, and the knee ached, but the longer he walked on it the less it hurt. By mid-afternoon he was walking almost normally, although the knee was still silently protesting.

His left hand was also stiff, but at least Patsy had kept it clean and it was free of any kind of infection.

The going was not hard at all. This path they were on seemed to simply wind around and around the mountain, taking them higher and higher. The men and the mule were able to negotiate it easily. The horses were able to walk, even though at times the path was a little too steep for them and their shoes would slide on the smooth rock floor.

At one point they all had to go single file. Clint took the lead with Duke, followed by Patsy with her horse, and then Schutz with his horse, and the mule. This was the first time in years that Clint found having Duke with him a disadvantage. The animal's size made the going even more difficult, and they finally reached a point when the horses just couldn't go any further.

"Now what do we do?" Schutz asked.

"We'll have to push on with the mule," Clint said. "It will be able to keep moving with us. I think the horses are done."

"Where do we leave them?" she asked.

"We'll look for a place."

As if it had been created by the gods for the horses, they found a small, flat plateau that actually had enough brush on it for them to feed for a while.

"A few days at most, probably," Clint said, "but hopefully that will be all we need."

Schutz and Patsy showed very little concern over the animals. It was only Clint who regretted having to leave Duke there.

"Take it easy, big boy," he told the big horse, his partner for many years. "I'll be back before you know I'm gone."

Clint read the look in Duke's eyes as one of trust, but the animal might just as well have been staring at him and thinking, "Look what you got us into this time."

THIRTY-EIGHT

They continued to follow the path, but in the late afternoon Schutz halted their progress.

"Look," he said, pointing to the finger peaks.

"What about them?" Patsy asked.

"They've moved," Clint said.

"Right," Schutz said.

"Mountains can't move," Patsy said.

"Right again," Schutz said.

"Then," Clint said, "*we're* moving."

"*Around* the damned things," Schutz added. "They were ahead of us, to our right, and now they're ahead of us to our left."

"That can't be," Clint said. "It must be . . . an illusion."

"Well, whatever it is," Schutz said, "there must be a way to get to them."

"Like what?" Patsy asked.

They all stood stock still while they considered the question. The only sound was the mule pawing at the ground and occasionally snorting.

"A cutoff," Schutz finally said. "There must be a cutoff *away* from this main path."

"If that's the case," Clint said, "then we must have missed it."

"Or," Schutz said, "it's ahead of us."

138

"So," Patsy asked, "what do we do?"

Again, it was a question they had to consider before they moved on—or back.

"I say we continue on," Clint said. "We might have missed one, but there might be another one."

"Why not go back?" Patsy asked.

"Because that's what we'd be doing," Clint said. "Going *back*. I think we should continue moving forward."

"I agree," Schutz said.

They looked at Patsy.

"Hey," she said, "I'm in your hands, remember?"

"Then let's go," Schutz said. "Maybe we'll find some sort of cutoff before dark."

As it turned out, they *did* find one, but not too long before dark.

It was a sliver, a separation in the rock wall to their inside. Oddly enough, it was Patsy who saw it.

"What's that?" she asked.

"What?" Schutz asked. He and Clint turned their attention in the direction she was indicating.

"There."

"I don't see anything," Schutz said.

"Wait," she said, and started walking along the wall with her hands pressed to it. Eventually, she found the opening and almost fell through.

"It's an opening, all right," Clint said, trying to peer inside, "but it's too dark to see where it leads to."

"So what do we do?" Patsy asked.

"It's dark inside," Schutz said. "We don't know what we're walking into."

"There's only one way to find out," Patsy said, and she stepped through.

"Patsy, wait!" Clint said.

"We'll have to go after her," Schutz said. He started to do so, but found that the opening was not quite big enough to accept his bulk.

"You'll have to turn sideways," Clint said.

"And even then it's a tight fit," Schutz said. He moved away from the opening and said, "You go ahead, Clint. If it's this narrow inside I might get stuck."

"All right," Clint said. "Better give me one of the torches."

Schutz took one of their two pitch-covered torches off the mule and handed it to Clint.

"Got matches?" the big man asked.

"I've got them."

"All right then," Schutz said. "Go ahead . . . but for Chrissake, be careful."

Clint took a deep breath, turned sideways, and slipped into the opening.

Patsy Kelly was in the dark, and it was cold. The sides of the passage she was in were freezing. In fact, they were damp as well. The chill was going right to her bone.

Up ahead all she could see was blackness, as if the tunnel she was in—she chose to *think* of it as a tunnel—was endless. At least if there was a light at the end . . .

She turned and looked behind her. She couldn't see any light that way either. The tunnel was probably winding. She felt a bolt of fear then. What if the tunnel had suddenly *closed* after she entered? What if Clint and Ben Schutz were banging on a smooth wall now, where once there had been an opening?

Should she go back? No. Then she'd have to explain her fear to them, and she would appear foolish. She decided to go on. This, then, would be her contribution to the expedition, to find out where this passage led—and hopefully it led *somewhere* and not just to some sort of . . . black . . . hole . . .

THIRTY-NINE

Inside the passage Clint quickly realized that it was more tunnel than anything else. Moving sideways, he was able to avoid touching the side walls. Schutz, if he came inside, would find it a tight squeeze, but he could probably force his way through.

As Clint continued on he realized that in order to light the torch he'd have to lift it over his head, because that was the only way he'd get the torch and the match close together. It was probably also a good way to set his hat—and head—on fire. He decided to leave the torch unlit until he got to a place where there was more room.

As he moved along he suddenly found himself able to face front. The passage was widening, which was good news for Schutz. The sides of the passage were cold and damp, but at least now he was able to avoid contact with them. Still, the chill coming from the walls was turning his blood cold—or so it felt. He turned and looked behind him, and found that the way was as dark as it was ahead of him. He decided it was time to light the torch.

He stopped, lit a match, and held it to the torch. As it blazed into life he was able to look around him, but there was nothing to see. The walls were bare and gray, although he could now see the moisture that beaded up on them and rolled down to the floor.

"Patsy," he called, and his voice echoed off the walls. He called again, this time louder, but there was still no answer. Could it be that the sound echoed for him, but before it went much further was swallowed up?

He continued on, holding the torch in front of him to light the way. He had no other choice, though. There were no turnoffs where he might have to decide which way to go; right, left, middle. It was just one continuous tunnel, and even without the torch he would have had to keep going forward.

Which was what he did.

Patsy turned. Was there someone behind her, or was she just imagining things? Had Clint and Ben Schutz followed her into the tunnel? She hoped so. She was starting to regret having been so impulsive. If only there had been *some* light to look at, or head for.

She looked behind her, and thought she saw some sort of a glow, but it wasn't the light she had been hoping for. Rather than some sort of white hole that might signify an opening, it was an eerie, flickering type of light. She decided to ignore it and just keep on going.

If she looked back it might be gaining on her.

Ben Schutz was undecided about what to do. He *thought* he might be able to squeeze through the opening, but what if it was no wider inside? What if it got *narrower* inside? What if he got *stuck*?

And then there was the mule to consider. The animal certainly wouldn't fit through, and what were they supposed to do with it? Just leave it there?

He decided that the best thing to do was just sit on the ground and wait for Clint to return. There was nothing else to do.

Clint moved along at a rapid pace now. The passage had widened still more, and the torch burned brightly. He didn't know how far into the mountain wall he had come, but at least he still seemed to be moving levelly or on a slight incline upward. He wasn't going back *down*.

He'd lost track of time. How long had he been wandering around in here? What was Schutz doing outside? And where was Patsy?

All of these questions swirled about in his head, along with the one that went, "Where was the gold?" Was it possible that *this* was where the gold was? Had they found it accidentally? Well, even if they had, he'd probably need Ben Schutz to verify it. Clint didn't know all that much about detecting gold in a mountain wall. He'd seen it panned in streams, and he'd even seen it dug out of rock walls, but he didn't know how to *spot* it.

Just for something to do, he held the torch close to the wall. All he saw was gray and black and *wet*. What were you supposed to see? Flashes of gold? He remembered that gold was usually very dull, not shiny the way most people thought it was. It was shiny after it had been cleaned and shined.

He stopped looking at the walls because it was an exercise in futility. Instead, he concentrated on where he was going.

It still looked like nowhere.

• • •

Patsy became excited.

She felt a breeze on her face, coming from up ahead of her. For a moment she thought she was imagining it, but she stopped and waited and there it was again, wafting by, tickling her face and hair.

A breeze, and on it the smell of fresh air.

She hurried towards it.

Clint was not as far along in the tunnel as Patsy was, but he detected the breeze about the same time she did. That was because the *torch* detected it, and the flame reacted, flaring slightly as the fresh air struck it.

If Patsy saw that opening and rushed to it, she might be rushing into a trap. It would be perfect for the man they were trailing to wait at the other end and just shoot at whoever came out of the tunnel. If that happened, the first person was going to be Patsy.

He quickened his already brisk pace.

Finally, Patsy saw the opening. She turned a corner and there it was. The tunnel was also lit by the daylight from outside. It had felt to her like she'd been in there a long time, and she was afraid that it would be dark outside when she found her way out, but obviously it wasn't.

She had made it all the way through, and even if this was a waste and was nowhere near the gold mine, she was just happy to finally have a way out.

She started to run, but as she neared the opening she heard something behind her, and then someone shouted, "Patsy! Wait!"

FORTY

Patsy turned, and relief flooded over her when she saw Clint Adams.

"Clint," she said, "you came after me."

"I should wring your pretty neck for you," he said as he reached her. "That was a foolish thing you did, rushing headlong into this tunnel. If there's a man with a rifle waiting outside, you would have been dead the moment you stepped outside."

She turned and looked at the opening with her eyes wide. "I didn't think—"

"No, that's right," he said, "you *didn't* think, right from the beginning."

"Clint—"

"Never mind," he said. "I have to go back and get Ben. I want you to *stay* right here. Don't step outside. Do you understand?"

"I understand."

Clint peered towards the mouth of the tunnel and said, "Even if we're in the wrong place right now, it's better than going in circles like we were." He looked at her again and said, "Stay here!"

"I'll stay," she said, "I promise."

"Ben and I will be back soon, probably after dark."

After dark? She tried to keep herself from panicking. When it got dark this *tunnel* would be dark.

As if he read the fear in her eyes he said, "Here, keep this torch. I'll put it out now, but you can light it again when it gets dark." He handed her the torch and the matches.

"Thanks," she said.

He regarded her for a moment, then hugged her tightly and said, "We'll be right back."

"Okay."

She watched as he went back through the tunnel and disappeared around a bend.

When Clint Adams reappeared Ben Schutz heaved a sigh of relief.

"Jesus," he said. "I didn't know what happened to you, and it's gettin' dark."

"I know," Clint said. "I caught up to Patsy and we found an opening at the other end."

"So you, uh, want me to come in?"

"It'll be a tight squeeze for about twenty or thirty feet, and then it widens out. You'll be all right."

"What about the mule?"

"No way the mule is going to fit," Clint said. "Let's just take a few supplies that we can carry and get moving. Patsy's waiting at the other end."

"What's *at* the other end?" Schutz asked.

"I don't know," Clint said. "I didn't stick my head out yet."

"Good idea," Schutz said. "You might have gotten it shot off."

"Come on," Clint said, and they unloaded some supplies from the mule, like blankets, coffee, and more matches and the second torch, as well as water canteens and the small pickax that Schutz had brought along. They left the mule loose and unencumbered, just in case it decided that it wanted to wander off.

"Ready?" Clint asked.

"As I'll ever be."

Clint stepped through the opening first, and then Ben Schutz did. He had to push hard, and the walls pressed against his front and back, but Clint was right. After about twenty or thirty feet he was able to turn and face front and follow close behind Clint.

FORTY-ONE

When the darkness fell, it came down over Patsy like a blanket. She sat on the cold, damp floor of the tunnel and lit the torch Clint had left her. The flame provided both light and a degree of heat. It also supplied a momentary relief from the fear she was feeling—but that quickly faded. Now, instead of fearing the dark, she found herself afraid of the flickering shadows tossed off by the flame.

She wished Clint would get back.

"How much further?" Ben Schutz asked.

"I don't know," Clint said uncomfortably.

"What do you mean, you don't know?" Schutz asked. "You just came this way."

"I know I did," Clint said, "but . . . I thought we'd be there by now."

"What?" Schutz said. "Are you saying this *isn't* the same tunnel."

Clint stopped, turned, and looked at Ben Schutz.

"I'm saying that's a possibility," Clint said.

"How did we get off into another tunnel?" the big man asked.

Clint shook his head and said, "Damned if I know."

Both men were silent for a few moments, both

thinking of Patsy Kelly, who was waiting at the end of that *other* tunnel. Who knows where *this* one would take them to?

"There's nothing else to do," Clint said finally, "but keep going."

Clint held the torch up at certain points so that Schutz could take a look at the rock walls. Once or twice the big man took some chunks from the wall to examine, but ended up shaking his head.

"Nothing here," he finally said.

"Well," Clint said, "that means we didn't find the gold by accident."

"We'll just have to keep looking," Schutz said, "for the gold and Patsy."

Clint nodded and they continued on.

Patsy was pacing the tunnel floor, from impatience *and* as a way to try to keep warm. She had found a crevice in the floor in which to wedge the torch, which now stood alone, still burning— but for how long? The pitch was starting to burn off completely, and soon she'd be left in the dark again.

Outside there was a dull glow, probably from the moon. Inside it would be as dark as a raven's wing soon. When that happened, she wondered if she'd be able to keep herself from seeking even the meager light the moon was giving off. Anything would be better than total darkness.

"I don't see an opening," Ben Schutz said.

"I feel it."

They had detected it before, thanks to the flare of the torch flame. Soon, they felt the air on their faces, and then finally saw the opening. There was just enough moonlight to discern it from the darkness around it.

"Is it the same?" Schutz asked.

"I don't know," Clint said. "When we get there, if Patsy's there, then it's the same one."

They headed for the opening, but Clint knew it wasn't the same. If it was, they'd have seen the torch that he had left with Patsy. Somehow, they had gotten turned onto another tunnel, and he wondered where *this* opening was in relation to the other.

Well, they'd soon find out.

FORTY-TWO

"Now what?" Schutz asked.

"It's dark," Clint said. "I guess we wait."

"What about Patsy?"

"She'll have to wait too."

"It's gonna get colder than this, Clint," Schutz said, "especially in a cave—and *we* have blankets."

"You're right," Clint said after a moment. Damn, but after all of this walking in damp quarters his knee was positively *killing* him. "I'll have to go and find her."

"You?"

"Well, of course. I left her there."

"You can hardly walk another step," Schutz said. "I'll go."

"Ben—"

"Clint," Schutz said. "you're not going to do us any good if you can't walk. Stay off that leg for a while. I'll find her."

Finally, Clint agreed. Schutz spread a blanket for him to sit on, but when Schutz started to go back the way they had come Clint called out.

"Ben?"

"What?"

Clint pointed to the opening that led outside and said, "That way."

Schutz turned. "Why that way?"

"Because you might get lost going back," Clint said, "and might end up in another tunnel entirely. Maybe—if we're lucky—all the tunnels go to the same place."

"You mean," Schutz said, "that she could be right next to us, but only if we go outside."

"Right."

Schutz thought a moment, then said, "You're right. There might be dozens of tunnels, but maybe they all come out in the same area."

Clint spread his hands and shrugged.

"Well, only one way to find out," Schutz said.

With the torch in hand Schutz moved to the mouth of the tunnel and looked outside.

"How does it look?" Clint asked.

"There's a ledge, but it's a wide one. I don't know what's further out, though."

"Just be careful."

Schutz stuck his head back in and said, "I'm gonna follow the ledge around and see if I can find some other openings. If I can, then one of them might be hers."

"Good luck."

"Be back soon."

Schutz withdrew his head, and was gone. Since Schutz had one torch and Patsy had the other, this left Clint Adams totally in the dark—in more ways than one.

Patsy couldn't decide what to do, but she was freezing. On the off chance that it might *not* be as cold outside, she decided to go out. Even if there was a man with a gun out there, surely he wouldn't be able to see her in the dark.

She took a deep breath and started for the mouth

of the cave. As she stuck her head out she looked both ways, and was surprised to see a torchlight moving towards her from the right. She withdrew her head quickly, and looked about for something to use as a weapon. Finally she found a rock that filled her hand, and it was the best that she could do. She flattened herself against the wall to the right of the opening and waited.

Schutz had tried three openings unsuccessfully. Inside he had looked all around, and now was fairly certain that although this mountain was probably a catacomb of tunnels, they all led to this center section. In the morning they'd be able to see a lot better and a lot more.

He came to the fourth opening and pushed the torch in ahead of him. If he hadn't, Patsy might have cracked him mightily on the head. As it was the rock struck him a painful blow on his wrist and he dropped the torch.

"Patsy!" he shouted. "Jesus, Patsy, it's Ben!"

"Ben?"

The torch, on the ground, remained lit, and as Ben Schutz stepped into the tunnel Patsy Kelly saw that it was him.

"Oh, God," she said, and threw her arms around him. Schutz stood there embarrassed for a moment, then shrugged and held her.

Schutz showed Patsy back to the tunnel where he had left Clint, and the three of them then huddled together with blankets around them. Clint and Schutz explained to Patsy what they thought they had found.

"But no gold," she said when they were finished.

"No," Clint said, shaking his head, "no gold."

"Well," she said, her eyes fluttering sleepily, "maybe tomorrow."

"Yeah, sure," Clint said, exchanging a glance with Schutz, "maybe tomorrow."

FORTY-THREE

In the morning Clint woke first and stretched his leg. The damned knee had stiffened up. He needed to get up and walk on it.

Sunlight streamed in through the tunnel mouth, bringing with it warmth. That had actually been what had awakened him. It had grown hot under his blanket, and he tossed it off and stood up.

He walked around in circles for a few moments, trying to work out the stiffness. Ben Schutz woke up and watched him for a few moments.

"How does it feel?"

Clint looked at the big man and shrugged. "Feels like shit."

"At least you're honest."

Schutz stood up and stretched, trying to work out the kinks in his back. Patsy was still asleep.

"Should we wake her?" Schutz asked.

"Not yet," Clint said. "Let's see what's outside first."

"I'll take a look," Schutz said, and he started walking towards the opening.

"Go easy, Ben," Clint said.

"I was out there in the dark, Clint," Schutz said over his shoulder. "You don't think I'm gonna

156

fall off in the daylight, do you?"

"That's not now what I mean . . . hey, hey, Ben!" Clint said. "Wait!"

But it was too late. Schutz walked right out through the opening, and the next thing Clint heard was the sharp crack of a rifle, and then Schutz was back into the tunnel, trying to catch his balance. Finally he fell before Clint could get to him.

Patsy came awake, and stared at Schutz as the man fell. She and Clint both saw the blood and knew he'd been hit.

"Ben!" Clint shouted. He rushed to the fallen man and knelt by him, ignoring the pain in his knee.

Patsy also moved to Schutz's side.

"Christ," Schutz said, "how stupid can I be? I *told* you myself yesterday—"

"Take it easy," Clint said. "Let me take a look at this."

The wound was in his left shoulder, and it didn't look too bad.

"We've got to stop the bleeding," Clint said. "The bullet will have to come out eventually."

"Get that bastard first," Schutz said. "That bastard who shot me. Get him."

Clint looked at Patsy and said, "Stop the bleeding."

"Where are you going?"

They were looking at each other across Ben Schutz's prone form.

"I'm going to do what Ben just asked me to do," Clint said. "I'm going to get that bastard."

Ken Hill pulled the trigger, and knew that he'd hit the man. He also knew that the man had been too big to be Clint Adams. That was all right. Now that he had found his mine, no one was going to take it away from him.

Since finding the mine he had been sitting there with a rifle, watching all of the tunnel exits around him. The walls opposite him and to his left and right were peppered with tunnels and openings. Luckily, there were none next to him in *his* wall, so he didn't have to worry about that.

He sat still now, watching the tunnel openings, keeping his rifle ready.

"What are you gonna do?" Patsy asked as she tried to stanch the flow of blood from Schutz's wound.

Clint checked the loads in his gun, then holstered it and picked up his rifle.

"I can't go out that way," Clint said, "so I've got to find another way. I have to go back the way we came and find another tunnel.

"You might get lost!"

"It's possible," he said.

She had successfully patched Schutz's shoulder, and Clint helped her drag him to a blanket. That done, he took Schutz's rifle and handed it to her.

"Just keep an eye on the mouth of the tunnel," Clint said, "in case he comes down after us."

"Do you think he will?"

"No," Clint said. "Figure he's got himself a nice perch somewhere and he's just going to wait for us to come out so he can pick up us off."

"And that's just what you're gonna do," she said. "You're gonna go out there and let him shoot you."

"I'm going out," he said, "but not to get shot. I'm going out to put an end to this once and for all."

"Sure," she said, "one way or another."

"No," Clint said, shaking his head, "I'll finish it my way."

He kissed her, put his hand on Schutz to make sure the man was still breathing, and then went back into the tunnel.

FORTY-FOUR

To Clint it felt as if he was moving around inside the same tunnel forever, but he finally found a new one and took it. He moved at a brisk pace, scraping himself a time or two on the jagged walls. By the time he found another opening, he was bleeding from several nicks on his face and arms, but he wasn't feeling any pain, not from the nicks and not from his knee or hand. He had one purpose in mind, and that was to finally get this sonofabitch who had been sending everyone else against him. It was time for them to meet man against man, with no one else between them.

He moved to the mouth of this new tunnel and looked out. He knew that the man with the rifle would be watching the same tunnel that Ben Schutz had come out of, but he'd also be alert for movement in the other tunnels. Clint decided that he was going to have to move quickly, and not just stroll out the way Schutz had.

He holstered his gun, because if he happened to slip on the ledge he was going to need both hands to save himself. Also, if he held the gun he might end up dropping it. As for the rifle, he had to leave it behind. It would only get in his way.

He inched toward the opening and tried to look outside, to get some idea of what was out there. Schutz had said there was a ledge that went all the way around, but there was no telling how wide the ledge was.

He also knew that once he was out there he was going to have to keep moving. He couldn't just go from tunnel mouth to tunnel mouth, because he'd rapidly lose his advantage. Once he was out there he was going to have to decide what his goal was, and he was going to have to *run* for it.

He rubbed his hands together, took a deep breath, and then sprinted out the tunnel mouth onto the ledge outside.

Ken Hill was taken by surprise. Even though he knew that Adams—or someone—might come out of one of the other tunnels, he didn't expect the man to come *running* out so fast. He brought the rifle to bear, and started firing in rapid succession, as quickly as he could, but he always seemed to be one step behind the running man. His bullets kept poking holes in the wall just behind the man.

"Damn," he muttered, but he kept firing until he couldn't see the man anymore.

If it was Clint Adams—and he was *sure* that it was—the man was now on the ledge *underneath* him.

Hill withdrew into his mine to await the Gunsmith's arrival.

As Clint broke out into the sunlight he got lucky. The sun reflected off metal, which had to be the shooter's rifle. Clint located it almost right away, and started running to his right, following the ledge. He *hoped* that the ledge would go all the way around and not just end.

He heard the shots, and knew that lead was poking holes in the wall behind him. Once or twice he felt the stone chips strike him on the back of the neck, but he kept running until he was directly underneath the shooter.

He flattened himself against the wall and took the time to catch his breath. He tried to locate the tunnel mouth where Patsy and Schutz would be, but he couldn't pick it out. Now he could see just how *many* of them there were. They dotted the entire wall face.

The wall he was leaning against was bare, however. There were no tunnel mouths here—but there had to be something. Otherwise, how had the shooter gotten up above him?

He decided to walk now, with his hands on the wall. There had to be an opening, even if it was like the one they had found into the original tunnel that had bought them here.

Just as they had found that one, suddenly his hands found emptiness in the wall, and there it was. Just a small opening, a sliver no bigger than the one the previous day. In fact, Clint doubted that Ben Schutz would be able to get through this one.

He could, though, by turning sideways, which he did. He took his gun out of his holster, held his hands straight out from his body so that the gun hand was ahead of him and his empty hand behind him, and went through the sliver opening.

He found himself in another tunnel, and followed it. Suddenly, it widened and he was in a cavern. This was different, all right. Instead of more tunnels, this one seemed to lead right into a cave—or was it a mine?

Was it *the* mine?

He didn't have time to think about that right now. The shooter was somewhere above him, and he had to find a way to get up there.

Ken Hill retreated well into what he was now thinking of as *his* gold mine. He crouched down and reloaded his rifle, then took out his handgun and checked the loads. That done, he simply settled down to wait.

FORTY-FIVE

There were several tunnels leading from the cavern he was in, but Clint found one that went up on a sharp incline, and he took that one. It was wide enough that he could walk normally, with his gun in his hand and ready.

Up the tunnel took him, up and up, until suddenly it leveled out. Here he had several choices once again, but why pick one? Why not just *ask* which one was the right one?

"Hello!" he called out.

No reply.

"This is Clint Adams," he called out. "I'm here, and I'm waiting."

No answer.

"I'm facing three tunnels," Clint said. "Let's get this over with so one of us can have this mine. Which path do I take?"

He waited, but there was still no answer.

"Come on," he called out, "or would you want me to come up walking backward, so you can have a clear shot at my back?"

He waited, and when he was about to give up a voice called out, "Take the tunnel on the right, it will lead you right to me."

"I'm on my way," Clint called out . . . and he took the tunnel to his *left*.

Ken Hill waited, watching the opening. As soon as Clint Adams showed his face he would fill it with lead, and the mine—the whole *mountain*— would be his.

He waited patiently, the hammer on his handgun cocked and ready. Suddenly he thought he heard something. Somebody's boots scraping on the floor . . . and then there was a voice from behind him.

"You didn't really think I was *that* stupid, did you?" the voice said.

"Shit," Ken Hill said. "You gonna shoot me in the back, Adams?"

"You've done your fair share of shooting from ambush, friend," Clint said, "and getting people killed, but no, I'm not going to shoot you in the back. Turn around."

"I'm turning," Hill said, "but if you shoot, this whole place will come down on us."

"*You* seemed willing to take that chance," Clint said. "So will I. Come on, turn!"

Abruptly, Ken Hill turned and threw himself prone. He rolled, hoping to get off a shot at Clint Adams even before he stopped moving, but he underestimated Adams's skill.

As the man started to roll, Clint picked out a point ahead of the man. It was something he did whenever leading a target. Pick a place where the target will go, not where it has come from, and be patient.

So he waited, and at just the right time he listened to his instincts and fired. He heard the bullet smack flesh, and the man stopped rolling and simply flopped over onto the ground and lay still.

Clint waited, listening and watching the ceiling of the mine. He had heard of cave-ins caused by loud noises, like gunfire, and now he waited to see if he would be the victim of one.

There was some rumbling, as if the ceiling *wanted* to come down, and then it stopped and things seemed to settle down.

He walked over to the fallen man, kicked his gun away from him, and checked him. He was dead, the bullet having struck him in the chest.

"You got what you want, friend," Clint said. "Here's your mine."

He left to go down and get his friends.

FORTY-SIX

It took a while for them to get up to the mine—days, in fact. They had to make Schutz comfortable, and then Clint had to dig the bullet out of his shoulder. After that, they gave him a couple of days to rest before Clint supported him—and he weighed a ton—and helped him up to the mine, with Patsy's help.

At one point Clint wondered if Duke was all right, but there was no way he could consider the horse's well-being over that of a man, no matter how long they had been together. He just had to hope that there had been enough feed to last the big gelding this long.

Finally, when they got up to the mine, Schutz told Clint what to do to bring him samples. They did *that* all day, and finally rested for dinner, which Patsy prepared from the last of their supplies.

"So?" Clint asked.

Schutz looked at him and said, "Nothing."

"What do you mean, nothing?" Patsy asked.

"I mean," Schutz said, "there are no indications that there is any gold in these walls."

"You mean," Patsy said, "it was *all* for nothing?"

"Looks that way," Schutz said. "Of course, there are some options."

"Such as?" Clint asked.

"I can stay and keep looking into this mine," Schutz said.

"Then this *is* a mine?" Patsy asked.

"It's *a* mine, yeah," Schutz said, "and there *might* be something here, if I keep looking."

"What's the other option?"

"That we keep looking for another mine."

Clint shook his head.

"That's not an option for me," he said. "I'm finished. I vote to head back."

"I vote to stay," Schutz said. "When I heal I'm going back down to get some supplies, and then I'll come back and keep looking."

"That's fine," Clint said. "Whatever you find is yours."

"Yours too," Schutz said.

"You don't have to do that," Clint said, "but if you want to give me a small percentage, I'll take it."

Clint looked at the woman and said, "Patsy?"

"Well . . . if Ben doesn't mind, I'd like to stay and help him."

"I could use the help," Schutz said, "and the company."

Patsy nodded and said, "I'm going to stay."

"Okay then," Clint said. "I'll head out in the morning."

Later, when Schutz was resting, Patsy came over to him and asked, "You don't mind?"

"No, Patsy," Clint said. "The decision is yours."

"I just figure I've come this far . . ."

"Sure," he said, "it makes sense. I wish both of you luck."

"I'll miss you," she said, leaning into him.

"Gold makes up for a lot," he said. "I hope you find it."

Late the next day Clint arrived at the point where they had left the horses. They were all there, looking somewhat skittish—except for Duke. The big gelding was standing over a bush that looked about nibbled out, and when Clint ambled over to him he gave him a baleful look that said, "Are we done here?"

"Yeah, big boy," Clint said, mounting up, "we're done here."

Watch for

VIGILANTE HUNT

139th in the exciting GUNSMITH series
from Jove

Coming in July!

J.R. ROBERTS

THE
GUNSMITH